Losing it

Losing It

M. Valentine Williams

Victorina Press
www.victorinapress.com

Copyright © 2022 by M. Valentine Williams
First published in Great Britain in 2022 by
Victorina Press
Wanfield Hall
Kingstone
Uttoxeter
Staffordshire, ST14 8QR
England

Typesetting and layout: Jorge Vasquez
Cover design: Triona Walsh

British Library Cataloguing in Publication Data
A catalogue record for this book is available from the
British Library.
ISBN: 978-1-9169057-6-4

Typeset in 11pt Garamond
Printed and bound in Great Britain by 4edge Ltd

One

Once there was a girl who grew up knowing that the choices she would make as an adult would be bad choices.

Sometimes there are no good choices.

Keep quiet and out of sight, pretend it's all right; that's one choice. Make a scene and fight, kick and scream all you want; that's another choice, but you'll only end up getting beaten or banged up. You see what I mean about choices?

There was a choice I had to make about the children. My children. I forget what it was now. It's why I'm here.

Back to this girl. She was all right, this girl. Took care of her mother and her younger sister. Tried her best to behave and be good; even her teacher praised her for trying her best. She liked her teacher. But even the teacher couldn't always see how tired the girl was, or how much she was worrying.

There was a grandmother as well, who was kind. This girl loved her grandmother, though she wasn't around for long enough to make a real difference. When she grew up, after all the bad things happened, it was another older woman who understood and took care of this girl. This woman's name was Elsie. She was a grandmother too.

This girl had a mother. She wasn't an orphan, or in care; she lived with her parents. But her mother wasn't able to help. She drank too much and the girl had to find food and cook for the family even when there was no money. She was only ten when the father left and the drinking really began. No wonder she and her sister clung together.

My name is Jane, by the way.

After her sister Michelle was taken away, the girl just wanted to escape, so when she met Fedo it seemed like a dream come true. He was good-looking, strong, knew how to take care of himself, and because he came from somewhere else he was very attractive to this girl. He paid attention to her, that was the important thing. He made her feel as though she was someone special. Everyone needs that. She had to make a choice – to go with him or to stay with her mother. She was sixteen. You have to understand that. She was sixteen. She chose to go with Fedo.

This girl I'm telling you about, she tried her best, but some things can't be mended. See, I'm crying now.

For the first time ever I'm making the right choice. This is my witness.

Robbie

When Jane was brought from the courts to this ward, we all wondered how she would cope with the other inmates. At first she didn't try to talk to them, just kept herself to herself in her room and slept a lot. That may have been the medication, but there again, she was very thin and looked as though she hadn't slept for weeks. All the residents here have tales to tell that would make your hair stand on end but we've learned not to let that affect how we treat the patients. We are careful, respectful and vigilant all the time, with each of our residents; at least I like to think we are. Jane was no different.

She was clearly psychotic when she arrived and out of touch with reality, but the drugs took care of some of that.

If you asked me what I meant by "psychotic", first of all I'd have to describe her as talking nonsense.

"When they come for me", she used to say, "I won't be able to stay here. I'm a celebrity, you know". She thought she was on a film set and that she was the star. She saw herself on TV and didn't understand it was our CCTV. She thought she was performing. Nothing about the reality made any sense to her, but her brain made up stories to fit what she thought was happening. It was sad to watch.

As time went on she calmed down, began to keep a diary and involve herself in the life of the ward. She began to draw and paint, and her work was, I suppose, an attempt to express some of the confusion and chaos that was in her head. It was rather beautiful, in a strange, alien sort of way. Mazes and interlocking shapes, lots of eyes and hands not attached to bodies – I found it a bit unpleasant to be honest, but other staff admired it, saying it was something called "outsider art" and quite fashionable.

There were some staff changes, and some of the keen young doctors and psychologists wanted to try out new approaches, which led to a certain amount of conflict between the nursing staff on the ward and the medics. At one point Jane got caught up in this when Dr Bruce tried out a new approach. I'm not sure we gave him much encouragement because her behaviour became more difficult to manage after each session.

I do feel we failed her though. I mean, life failed her, her parents failed her, God knows social services failed her, and in the end we couldn't help her either, even though we wanted to. We amalgamated with another special hospital and we were too busy keeping afloat in the upheaval caused by that to pay as much attention as was needed to our individual patients.

She was attached to Trevor, one of the charge nurses, but he left and that upset her a lot. That was the first time she seriously tried to end her life.

Jane will be missed, but mainly by the staff here, which says a lot. I'm not even sure if the man she lived with knows she's dead.

Elsie

I know Jane had a strong attachment to me and I must admit I did wonder how she'd cope after I retired. We don't encourage the patients to get too dependent on us, but it still happens.

I was the one who found her and brought her back. I sometimes think it might have been better if I hadn't. Poor kid.

She never got a straightforward diagnosis. I think we all just accepted that circumstances had made her who she was. That's true for most of our patients – crap in, crap out, as Trevor used to say. He's right. Even the disturbed and dangerous characters like Henry weren't born that way.

I feel sad when I think about what happened, but in a way it's the only way it could have turned out. For her, the agony is over. Perhaps we did give her something. A taste of humanity and kindness, if nothing else. Bruce thought he could cure her. What I think he did, unwittingly, was to break down the wall between what happened in the past and the present.

Recollecting and re-living her childhood, and what happened later, restored her sanity, but knowing the reality also drove her back into a place she couldn't escape from, except by doing what she did.

Dr Bruce

I owe Jane a lot. It's not easy being a psychiatrist, and patients aren't always co-operative, but there was something about Jane that made me want to try and reach her without all the drugs, to see whether she could be restored to the point of being able to leave the hospital. It has happened before.

Elsie was right though, I should have approached her much more carefully. Now I've read all the notes – stretching back over her whole life, near enough – I am angry that she wasn't given the care she needed earlier. But I tried, I really did.

Reading her journals has been an eye-opener for me.

Although I think we become hardened to horrors other people wouldn't even begin to cope with, we do still burn out. Treating each and every patient as an individual and trying to understand what's going on for them in their world, however distorted or alien it might look to us, is exhausting over any length of time. We are bombarded with demands for our time and attention, but we do the best we can.

Some patients do get to you. We're not robots, and personally I'm glad that I still have enough humanity and feeling left to mind when someone I've known as a patient takes a turn for the worse, or opts out altogether. Who could blame them? Suicide may be the sanest response to a crazy world.

But Jane, poor old Jane, she might have had a chance to leave here, if she'd been properly supported. I did get through to her, I know I did, but the kind of therapeutic treatment I was advocating has to be supported by the staff and the powers that be above them. I thought I was so clever, working with her in the way I did, but all I did was to make matters worse. Or did I? I'm not even certain of that any more. She was lucid, coherent and rational when I saw her last, but she'd made up her mind.

I think the quiet meditation room was her favourite place, judging from her journals. She felt able to be herself there. Able to let go of a lot of stuff we never knew about. Trevor was responsible for that room. He put forward the idea at a meeting and we had some reservations. Even with surveillance it seemed a little risky, given what some of the patients do when they're ill.

We couldn't trust Jane in there either at first, but we learned to let go and have faith in her – you have to, sometimes – and she responded by being trustworthy. Of course it didn't happen overnight. She was quite ill when she arrived and it took time for all of us to see what she was going to be like.

What was she like? Touching, childlike, tragic in a way, provocative, unpredictable at times – all of that. There was something about her that made you want to help her. We all tried. Sometimes things don't work out the way they should.

Losing It

Two

Trevor unlocks the door and lets me into the room. He keeps the keys. My room. My special room. I look round, remembering it.

This space has been made comfortable with the addition of my own things: a cushion, a throw-over, a large beanbag, and the little pink light that glows like the inside of a shell, softly lighting one corner. Here is where I come to meditate, in this rosy light, on this floor, with this beanbag to prop up my spine. The rug is thick and comforting.

I remove my shoes and sit in the posture: spine erect, hands lightly open and resting on my thighs. There is a slight scent of potpourri, mainly lavender, which they tell me is calming. They encouraged me to take up meditation, thinking that it might help soothe my troubled soul. As it's unlikely they'll ever let me leave, I mostly go along with what they want.

When I come in here, I sign in with Howard, so they know where I am. I've been coming into this room for almost two years now and they only had to come and get me out once, just after I started. Things were bad then; as soon as I was left alone anywhere I felt anger overtaking me. I ripped open the beanbag – they said I was "frenzied", whatever that means – and stuffed the polystyrene beans into my mouth. I nearly choked myself, which was what I intended of course. Now there are lots of things I could kill myself with, but I don't always want to any more. I'm not sure if they still watch me while I'm in this room; I know they used to, through the camera in the corner.

You have to do something pretty bad to be in here. Take Thomas. He looks meek and mild enough, but when a new staff member came who didn't know him too well, they let him go to the toilet on his own. Thomas poked his own eye out and then started screaming. Such screaming! Everyone came running and luckily one of the nurses knew what to do. Thomas's eye was put back, but it doesn't look quite right.

These things often happen here. I know. I've done things too. And when they happen I feel disgusted, but excited at the same time. That's how it still is – though Robbie says I am making good progress. Well, I don't know about that, and what does it matter? I'm here for life anyway. I talk to the others sometimes, but I won't talk about what happened, why I'm in here; it's not important, not to me anyway. It was all a long time ago, and I wasn't responsible. Diminished responsibility they said, which is another way of saying I was mad, crackers, loony – a homicidal maniac in fact. I keep myself to myself, and as long as the bit on the outside looks okay they don't question me much.

Be still, be calm. Meditate.

I look at myself in the mirror sometimes (plastic, shatter proof) and I don't recognise the person I see there. Long dark hair, which they've allowed me to grow; thin face; big eyes with dark circles under them; sallow skin. That's me. I've been away from the outside world for twelve years and the woman I see in the mirror isn't me.

The real me is somewhere else, wearing an up-to-date tracksuit and trainers, and with a ponytail. She is twenty-two and free, while the woman I see in the mirror is thirty-something, and looks anything but free. In my dreams I see myself as I was then, doing what I did then. I'm not telling what that was. They know, it's all written down somewhere in a file, all the court reports or whatever.

Breathe deeply. Relax. Let all the outside stuff disappear. Here there is real freedom. Let me be silent, let me concentrate. The voices, impulses, or whatever you call them, are quiet. The medication has quietened them, as they said it would. I centre myself, breathe deeply and relax. I lose myself in my own private kingdom.

"Sometimes I live in the country
And sometimes I live in the town
And sometimes I take a great notion
To jump in the river and drown."

The water laps around my body, drawing it this way, tugging it that way. My hair streams out in the currents, my legs and arms are weightless, floating, adrift in the blood-warm sea, buoyant in the liquid quicksilver night.

Phosphorescence in the water, stirred up by the motion of my body, glimmers in translucent droplets, the palest green, like liquid fire. My fingers extend into the enfolding darkness of the ocean, gentle breaths of foam curl and slide, the tides surge on below me. Take me with you, absorb me, assimilate me, draw me to you. I want to be joined, to belong, to be one. One.

Meditate. Float. Relax.

Three

The ward staff, in their regulation uniforms, are always on watch. Robbie and Trevor, the two charge nurses, write up their notes in the logbook. Trevor glances frequently at the black and white monitor in the corner, which shows a small grey figure sitting cross-legged in a small grey room. The figure is unmoving, looks insignificant on the small screen, but they watch her carefully, all the same. Robbie – dark, thin and a worrier – wonders if he'll be late again for his young daughter's birthday party. His wife will be angry with him if he's late, and the way things are going his marriage could be in trouble. He wants to do his best to make things right, but this job doesn't make it easy.

'Jane's been a long time in the quiet room. Everything all right, Trevor?'

'Yeah – I've got a clear view. She's just sitting there. Seems fine.'

'Give her another ten minutes max, then hoick her out, Trev, okay?'

'No problem. Ken can watch the screen while I get her if you want to go off home.'

'Good idea. Thanks. I did say I'd be back for Molly's birthday tea if possible. See you tomorrow then.' Robbie's shoulders sag with the efforts of the day. He undoes the safety lock and heads for the fresh air, handing in his keys as he passes security.

'Ken, can you take over for a bit while I get Jane back?' asks Trevor.

Ken, who has been outside the office watching two male patients finish a game of chess, positions himself so that he can watch the chess players and the monitor.

'No problem. How's she doing?'

'Hard to tell. She seems so normal, but it's anyone's guess what goes on inside that head. Remember Daphne's doll?'

'Certainly do. You get used to most things in this job, but sometimes things still get to you. Yeah, I remember that incident very well. Poor old Daphne.'

'You okay while I go and get her?'

'Sure.'

Trevor walks with his usual bouncy stride towards the quiet room. There is lino on the floors, and there are recessed lights, calming pastel decor, no curtains, safety bars on windows. He passes through these areas wishing – as always – that he were somewhere else. Tables and chairs bolted to the floor in the dining area, armchairs which have been picked to death on their arms; it's not a good working environment, but for some people it's home. Trevor hopes he won't be around there much longer, he has plans to move on. Unlike the residents, he has somewhere else to go.

Four

Is my time up already? It doesn't seem like I've been in here more than a minute. Go away, Trev, let me sit here a while longer. Can't argue, they'll only put me in the holding room and I haven't the energy this afternoon to cope with all that. Smile at Trevor sweetly and get up slowly, so as not to startle him. Trevor's all right, as good as anyone else working here. None of them really understand. I hope we've got something decent for supper and not the usual muck we've been having lately. They say it's because the food bill has to be cut, but I think the cook has left and they're making do with a temporary chef, who doesn't know what we like.

Some of the tranx leave your mouth sore and dry, so it's no good eating scratchy or rough food. You may crave meat – a nice juicy steak – but you'll never get it here, unless it's mince. No wonder I'm anaemic. Stodge and starch is what we get, and the way some of them eat would make you sick if the food didn't.

'I'm coming, Trevor, I'm coming.'

Losing It

Five

Four to a table they sit, wrinkling their noses at the smell of cabbage and mashed potato. Ken serves the male patients first, family style.

'Ken, why does Thomas always get the first helping?'

'I don't know, Jane. It seems to be important to him. Does it matter?'

'It doesn't matter, it's just that it always happens. Why can't someone else get the first helping?'

He tries to change the subject. 'Did you do your meditation today, Jane? How's it coming along?'

'Thomas is a madman.' Jane glances at Thomas, to gauge the effect.

'Now come on Jane, don't wind him up. I asked you how you got on today.'

'I got on very well until I sat down with Thomas the madman.'

'Jane, stop now. Or you'll miss your supper.' Ken's face is set. He stands no nonsense.

'It's so scrumptious, too, isn't it? You'd have to be mad to miss supper, don't you think, Thomas?'

'Jane!'

'I'm going.' She scowls and leaves the table.

Trevor comes over. 'I'll write it up in the book, Ken.'

'Thanks, Trevor.' Ken turns away, studiously ignoring Jane. It's like this every day, sometimes worse; all the aggression that these patients feel is locked up here with them. It has to leak out somewhere.

Six

I concentrated today, really concentrated, and I could feel a layer of me being removed, like the skin of an onion. It was very strange. I started to meditate, to focus, and Thomas came into my mind, always having to be fed before anyone else. I saw my father sitting there instead of Thomas, demanding his tea. He was about Thomas's age, and we all gave in to him because we couldn't face a fight about it. It was easier to let him have his way. We had no choice; at least that's what I believed at the time. I know differently now.

Nothing's changed, but as I say, a tiny little layer has been removed and I am a bit raw where I was reminded of our father. I am travelling inwards, slowly, on a journey to freedom.

Maybe.

During their break, Ken chats with Elsie, who has special responsibility for Jane. Elsie is not sure what's bothering her, but she airs her thoughts anyway. She speaks carefully, her lined mouth puckering to meet the warm, sweet coffee.

'Jane seems strange today. I can't quite put my finger on it, but there's something not quite right.'

'When is she due for review?'

'Next week. The doc thinks her medication's all right; I asked him. Personally, I'm not sure how you tell – unless she blows, of course.'

Ken nods. 'I'll mention it again at the staff meeting.'

He usually chairs these meetings and is happy with the role. Elsie knows the psychiatrists would rather listen to Ken and Trevor. She's tired of fighting the system and lets them get on with it now.

'Would you? See if anyone else has noticed anything odd about her? Thanks.'

'She seems to be spending a lot of time in the relaxation room at present. Is that a bad thing, do you think?

Does she need more time with other patients?' Ken asks. He puts his coffee down and stretches, yawning widely. He is looking forward to the end of the shift.

'Who knows? But I'll keep a more detailed diary if you like, just to be on the safe side.'

Elsie knows Jane better than anyone, but she doesn't know everything.

Seven

I used to see Mr Stone on a Tuesday, but he's seeing someone else now. It's a pity, but they felt I couldn't be trusted with art materials then. I sharpened the metal ring holding the bristles in my paintbrush and cut a nice big circular chunk out of my arm. Just like that! It didn't hurt at all. Afterwards, Mr Stone said he was very worried about me. Too late, as usual. A pity. I used to enjoy those sessions.

Trev stinks of fags. I could kill for a ciggie, but we're not allowed them are we? We might set the place alight or something.

Time for the evening drug round.

'Jane, how are you sleeping at present? Do you want a tab?'

'No thanks, Ken.' I know my eyes are heavy and dark ringed, but that's normal for me.

'Okay. As long as you're sure.'

He leaves, goes to see Thomas and Henry at the other end of the ward. I remain on my chair, in my tiny room, and stare into space.

Losing It

Eight

Sleep. Yeah, it's hard to get a good, peaceful night's sleep. I sleep, but I wake up feeling tired. It's slightly better than all those years before, when I was afraid to drop off in case you-know-what happened. If there was a row going on, someone getting beaten up, you'd hear it and wake up, but with you-know-what he was always sneaky and dead quiet. Ha, that's funny – dead quiet. He is now anyway. Pity he didn't go sooner, he would have spared us a lot of bother. The trouble is, when someone's dead you haven't got them there to be angry with any more. You still feel angry as hell, but what good does it do you?

Time to go and wash. Elsie will watch me; she's a tough old bird but she and I have got to know one another well over these years. I think she's a lezzie, but she doesn't bother me.

'Hi, Elsie.'

'Hello, Jane. Time to wash. Is it hair shampoo night?'

'Yes, it's that new one they bought, the other one makes my head itch.'

'And we can't have that can we?' She rummages in the drawer, pulls out the shampoo and locks it again. 'Is this the one you want to use?'

'That's it. I think I've got everything.'

The water pours around my head from the shower. I refuse to have a bath because of feeling scared. They might push my head under the water. When I go in a bathroom, memories come back of terrible things: that locked room, the water filling the tub, me with no clothes on. I only had a little voice then; we all did.

The shower's okay; I can manage the shower.

Elsie waits quietly and hands me the towel when I finish. She rubs my hair dry like I've seen mothers do with their children. She uses big, pink, soft towels, not like usual hospital stuff. I insisted, and they bought them for me, just me, to use. I put my bathrobe on and look at myself in the mirror.

I had a mother once who looked at me. I knew her face; I smiled when she smiled, cried when she cried, cried when she got angry. It seems that somewhere I have a memory of this, but I can't find it. Meditate. Maybe it will come.

Elsie is like a mum to me. She dries my hair, inspects my nails; she treats me with respect. Grandma Elsie. Suddenly I give her a kiss on the cheek. She jumps back, surprised.

'Jane! What was that for?'

'Sorry, Elsie. I was just thinking.'

'Thinking what?'

'You're sort of, kind of, a bit like my mum, being there and drying my hair and everything.'

'So, I'm a bit like your mum, am I? I'm probably not far off her age either. I've never heard you mention your mum before.'

'I don't much. She died. I didn't really know her for many years.'

'That's sad. It's hard not to have a mum around.'

'Is your mum still alive?'

'She died last year. Do you remember I was off for a while in March? She was a very old lady and she died suddenly. She had a good life, but we were sad to see her go. So you and I are orphans then, Jane?'

'Yes, we're orphans.'

That's strange. Elsie and I are orphans. Orphans. I never thought about that before.

Nine

Meditating. Becoming calm and centred. Breathing slowly and deeply. In and out, in and out. Slowly. No gentle sea today.

Images swirl in my mind. I see a chaotic whirl of colours, and in the middle is my star. The galaxy wheels and turns, purples and blues, streams of indigo and sepia trail around my star.

Concentrate. Focus on the star. It's too far away and all this whirling madness gets in the way. I can't think, can't focus. The room has gone cold. Has Trev turned off the heating by accident? I have been cold before, many many times, hiding at night. There was no heating in that house. My bed was wet, and so cold. Michelle was a baby then, a tiny little baby. I had to look after her in the night when she woke. We snuggled together for warmth. Where is she now? Still with that revolting husband, I bet. I wouldn't speak to her once I found out about him and his tricks. She still wouldn't throw him out.

Here comes Trev.

'Jane, I've come to fetch you. The heating boiler's up the spout and it'll be cold while they fix it, so I thought I'd better come and get you. You can go in the visitor's room with the others if you're cold, there's heating in there.'

'It's okay, Trev, I'll go to bed.'

'Elsie hasn't come on shift yet, Jane, so you'll have to wait a while. Jane?'

'I can hear you.'

'I thought you were going to have a tantrum.'

'Well I'm not.'

Trev worries about me. His mild, pale face is lightly creased, his blue eyes searching me for signs. He's seen me do things. He knows what I'm capable of.

At night the bad things come out, dark wicked shadows with knives that laugh. But I go to bed anyway.

Ten

A figure creeps along the corridor. It has no face, but it is evil. Wickedness walking, holding a knife. Dark, angular shape. Walls will not hold you back, doors will not keep you from me.

The babies! The babies! Where are they? I must protect them, cover them with my body. Now, now, now. Oh my God, where are they? Please, please, where are they?

Lights.

'Jane? What's the problem? You're waking the other residents.'

'I thought . . . I thought . . . it's the same dream again. Can I have the light on for a bit?'

'Do you want something to help you sleep? I can get you something.'

'It keeps trying to kill them. Horrible. Horrible.'

'Kill who, Jane? Wipe your eyes now.'

'The babies. It keeps trying to kill the babies.'

'You were having a bad dream, Jane. It's over now. Go back to sleep.'

They won't talk about the babies. Oh, they know about them all right, but they're afraid of upsetting me. Poor, poor, babies. It might come back if I go back to sleep. Sit up and keep vigil in the dark. Meditate. The pin I found on the floor is in my hand.

The rivers run under the earth, searching for a way out. They come to the surface, bubbling clear and pure, wanting release. Let the water out. It flows, blood red, crimson flowers exploding. My own poppy fields. Calm, numb, chilled out; let me float away, float away.

'Jane! Oh my goodness. Andy, get down here quick. It's Jane. She's cut her wrists. No. I'll dial the doc. Hurry.'

'Only a very faint pulse. When did you last look in?'

'Two-fifteen. She was having a bad dream, but she seemed to settle again.'

'Keep the pressure on the wound. She'll need a transfusion I think. Where's the doc?'

'Coming. Right, let me look at her. What a mess. Can you hold her arms while I put these on? Then we can get her on the stretcher. Okay. Andy, can you warn them we'll need some blood? Right, young lady, let's get you sorted out.'

Suddenly it's all sorted out. Everyone knows what to do; it's what they've been trained for.

White against the whiter sheets, my arm is still. Dirty-yellow white, with bluish veins like sour milk pulsing just below the skin. I am floating again, on my bed boat, into unknown lands, sliding over the oceans; my eyes are closed. I do not want to come back; there is no pain where I am, no remorse, no hunger, fear or thirst, only the timeless ocean surging, spinning me, rocking me, slowly on its crest. Let me go, let me go.

'Hello, Jane. Feeling better?'

'Go away, Trev.'

'That's no way to talk when I've come all the way from the ward to see you.'

'Sorry, Trev.'

'So you should be, giving us a fright like that.' He doesn't look offended.

'I couldn't help it. I don't want to be here. I'd rather be dead, don't you see?'

But he doesn't see. None of them do. The psychiatrist came to see me this morning. His eyes twinkled kindly, but I can't talk to him. Am I mad? I don't know. What is madness anyway? I feel sad, not mad, and there's no treatment for that. He wants me to talk to someone, but what good would it do? It won't get me out of here.

Elsie came to see me tonight before she went home. She held my hand for a minute, but she didn't say much. Elsie and I are orphans. She understands.

Eleven

'Jane! Someone to see you. Come to the lounge when you're ready.'

'Okay.'

I wonder who it is. No one has come to visit me for a long time. I go through a list of possible visitors: Father Dominic, Aunt Olive, a new social worker, some health official on a fact-finding mission, a research student from the Psychology Department. I don't want to see anyone. I'm too weak. It was only three days ago that I had a blood transfusion and I'm still wobbly. I look in the mirror as I go out – hair neat, eyes dark-ringed, skin sallow. It's much as you would expect.

'Hello, Jane. Thank you for agreeing to meet me.'

Huh! I wasn't even asked. But since I'm here I'll play the game. 'That's okay.'

Robbie keeps an eye on me from the corner. I have to watch my manners.

We sit down. I look at him, up and down. He seems a bit unnerved by my scrutiny, but he sits there, waiting for me to be ready.

'Jane, Dr Khan asked me to pop in and see you. My name's Bruce Townsend. I'm taking over from John Dooley as Registrar.'

I go blank. I've never heard of John Dooley. Usually the registrars don't come near us, they stay safely where they belong with the ordinary madmen out there, dispensing medicines and asking their stupid questions. This one seems to have escaped.

'How do you do, Dr Townsend?' Nice manners. This surprises him.

'I wonder if it would be okay for us to meet from time to time, Jane? I'm trying out some new ideas and I need someone like you to help me. All it will involve is talking, and you don't have to say anything if you don't want to. I'd like to meet you four or five times, to ask you some questions, and if you'll think about some things for me. What do you think?'

I keep silent. It makes him uncomfortable, but I'm not here to make life easier for him.

'When do you want to start?'

'Tomorrow? How would three-thirty be?'

'Robbie?' He nods.

So it's settled then. Bruce. Funny name. He's not even Australian, or Scottish. The day drifts on. I have no nightmares.

Twelve

Meditate. They've let me come back in here today, but they've told me they're watching in case I do something silly. Something silly! If only I could. They always find out and whisk me away to safety. But I don't want to go. Can you will yourself to die? What if I stopped breathing? No, I tried that once and as soon as you pass out you start breathing again, automatically. Bruce's face comes into my head. I'm due to see him again tomorrow.

It was strange being in a room with him on my own; he was very careful about how far away from me he sat, I could tell the others had warned him about not upsetting me.

It's cold outside today and the sky is pale pale blue.

"Brightness falls from the air,
Queens have died young and fair.
Dust hath closed Helen's eye
I am sick, I must die,
Lord have mercy upon us."

If only I could die. The words keep haunting me, the words from the old poetry books I had in school. Brightness falls from the air – it could fall today, like silver dust, like moonbeams in the day, like frost flowers on a frozen pool. Brightness. But I won't be there to see it. I am in here, and I fret, I yearn, I long to be free. Queen Jane, dead on arrival, brightness fell on her and she died. Man cannot stand too much brightness falling from the air.

The poster on the wall seems different today, the colours look wrong and the angles seem so sharp, like prisms. The focus is too intense. It's the new tablets I expect. It all looks far away and distorted, like crazy paving. Ha! I am getting angry. They're watching me. I pull the shirt I'm wearing over my head, so they can't look. There's no privacy at all.

'Jane!'

It's Trev. I'm not surprised, I knew they'd come and get me.

'Jane – pull your shirt down. Come back into the main ward, now.'

I remain silent. I do not move. I stop breathing.

'Jane! Come on – don't try to do anything silly.'

Oh no, mustn't try anything silly, must we? Not silly like strangling babies, or setting fire to the house. Not silly like some of the others, not silly like cutting my arms.

Or my throat.

Thirteen

Thirteen – ah yes, thirteen. Do I need the bad luck of thirteen? What else can happen?

Trev has left the hospital. Went for another job and got it – didn't want to say goodbye.

Bastard. Bastard. Bastard.

I hug my blanket, stay in bed; I don't want to come out. Robbie comes to see me.

'I know, Jane, it's tough. You'd got used to Trevor. We'll all miss him here, but these things happen. I'm still here, so are Ken and Elsie. It's okay.'

Robbie smiles at me, but I'm not fooled. It's not okay. And Elsie will retire before long and then I'll have no one.

I don't want to talk to Dr Bruce; I don't want to talk to anyone. I talk nonsense, as a way of escaping his questions. Tweedle tweedle deedle deedle I go, rumpty umpty empty teddy, and he sits and watches me silently, his large brown eyes registering concern. Then he speaks.

'Teddy is empty? Your teddy?'

Startled, I nod.

'Peedle poodle windle bondle makepiece. Marble. Shit.' I run out of words.

'Empty teddy, babbytears, pagga points, blubba eyes,' he replies in kind. I am startled by his joining in what I had thought was rubbish. He goes on. 'You feel like shit because Trev's got another job. You feel empty and sad, but you can't cry?'

Where did that come from? How did he guess?

My hands come up to my face and rake across my eyes. I can't cry. The tranx have made me dead, killed the tears. Gently, he touches my hands.

'Don't hurt your face, Jane,' he says, smiling.

A very small voice comes out of me. A little girl's voice, one I haven't heard before – or not for many years.

'Jane's crying.'

He repeats this. 'Jane's crying. Jane's very sad. Poor little Jane.'

He opens a bag and brings out some things. One of them is a girl doll. He puts it on the table, wrapped in a blanket.

'Poor baby doll, you're crying and we don't know how to make it better.'

My little girl voice tells him that it's never going to be better. 'Dolly's dead.'

He is silent, thinking. He got too close too soon.

I snatch the doll away from him and hold it by its legs while I swing it viciously, beating its head against the table top. He does not try to stop me. Outside the door, Robbie, who is waiting, looks concerned. Dr Bruce catches his eye and warns him off with a little gesture of his hand.

'This is a baby who has been badly hurt,' he says, 'so badly hurt she may even be dead.'

He falls silent. I feel, for the first time, tears forming at the back of my eyes. I blink hard to hold them in. Our time together is up. Robbie opens the door. Dr Bruce doesn't say anything; he looks serious and thoughtful. But I shall meet him again on Thursday.

Fourteen

The staff arrive at different times for the review meeting. They fetch cups of coffee from the machine, which dispenses hot, dark liquid into plastic cups, too hot to hold. Bruce decides against having a drink, he's keyed up enough as it is without the buzz of extra caffeine.

When he put himself forward for this project he had some ideas about how he wanted to work with these patients. Even personality-disordered people must have feelings somewhere inside them, he believed. If only one could tap into that – bring them alive – one might get somewhere. He muses over his last session with Jane as he waits for Robbie and Ken to finish organising their cover for the meeting. His use of nonsense babble in response to Jane was something he'd read about in Erickson, but when it emerged spontaneously in the session he had wondered afterwards what impact it might have had. What would the staff make of it?

The others come in and sit down. Ken glances at them, shrewdly assessing their views. Robbie is staring uneasily at his fingers; Elsie is hunched in her chair, staying out of the way. Howard, on duty outside, has already made his feelings known. Andy, out of touch with events, looks round with interest. There is tension in the air. He doesn't know where it is coming from, but he doesn't have long to wait.

'Thank you for coming to this meeting, Bruce.'

'I just hope I can help. Did you read my memo about the project? I thought it might explain things a bit.' He looks round hopefully, but the others fix their gaze on their fidgeting hands.

Ken decides not to beat about the bush. 'Bruce . . . I don't know how to say this, but we're not altogether happy about this project of yours.' He coughs. There is a silence.

Bruce glances at the other staff members. They avoid his eyes.

'Oh. I see. Can you tell me what it is you're worried about?'

'Jane has been stable here for a long time now. We understand her moods, her ups and downs, and Elsie and Robbie have a good relationship with her. Now that Trevor's left, Jane seems upset, and we feel she might try cutting herself again. She made an attempt not so long ago to hurt herself – just before you arrived, actually – and we have concerns about her care and general welfare. Dr Khan has changed her medication recently, because there were indications she was becoming psychotic again. All in all, we feel it's the wrong time to be offering her this kind of therapy. If I'm honest, I have some worries about exactly what you're doing with her.'

There is a silence, broken by noises from outside the nurses' room; someone is protesting about the food, loudly and plaintively.

Bruce thinks hard. 'Before I met Jane, we went over all the background details very carefully, and she met the exact criteria for the study. She comes willingly to our meetings, doesn't she?' They nod, reluctantly. 'Of course that might be because it breaks up the week a bit and gives her something to think about.'

Too late he realises what he's said.

'I think that's the point, Bruce. She broods. We don't know what she's brooding about, she won't speak to us properly, but this gives her one more thing to worry over. That means caring for her becomes more difficult – you must see that.'

'I do, but is it reason enough to stop her coming? Of course I recognise the difficulty for you, but treatment of any sort can alter the status quo, make life more difficult for a while. No reason not to try it, though.'

The staff members look sceptical.

Ken breaks the silence. 'Can you tell us something about your approach? If you're asking us to support you in this, then you should at least let us know what you're doing.'

'Sure, I've no secrets. I am almost a beginner at this, and I have to admit that with all honesty. Initially, I aim to step into her world, to get alongside her so to speak, to help her trust me. She nearly cried the other day – that's a breakthrough as far as I can see.'

The staff look unsure about whether this is an advance.

'Why is that a breakthrough?' asks Robbie.

'Has she cried before?'

'She's quite secure here; she gets on well with the staff. She's had no need to cry.'

'But she wants to die, doesn't she? She thinks about death a lot?'

'Yes, but when you've done the kind of things she's done, you know you're not going to get out. What's the point of crying over it? I'd rather be dead than have to spend the rest of my life in here with the likes of some of them. Jane's normal in comparison.' Robbie leans forward to emphasise his words.

'I don't seem to be getting through,' Bruce replies. 'Can we agree to disagree? I would like to carry on seeing her now we've started. It's early days, after all – I've only seen her twice. How about if we review the situation in two months? By then we should know more clearly if it's going to help her, and if we can deal with the problems it causes.'

They fix some dates in their diaries. Ken goes away to check out the credentials of Dr Bruce Townsend, knowing he will have to tackle the consultant psychiatrist, Dr Khan, if Dr Townsend won't go quietly. He'll bide his time.

Bruce, disconcerted and uneasy, takes himself off into the car park to have a smoke. He needs to think about this. Dr Khan is old fashioned in his views about patient care; he will need to put his side across first before Robbie or Ken can interfere.

In the hospital staff canteen he meets Joseph, who is having a hard time with a group of anorexic girls on Ward 12.

'How's life, Joe?'

'Pretty shitty, since you ask. How about you?'

'Just come back from a meeting with the staff in the Special Unit. They made me feel like I was some quack without the first idea about anything. "Give up working in mental health now" seemed to be the message. I mean, if you don't try a new approach, how can you ever learn what might work? Bunch of tossers.'

'I thought you said you had great respect for the way they did a difficult job and handled the patients.'

'I do, in a way, but they're so conservative. I tried to explain what I was doing, but they just stared at me blankly, like I was some kind of patient talking gibberish at them. Very disheartening.'

'Well, I've just had a horrendous morning with Ward 12. Three of them have made some kind of pact. We're going to have to intervene if they don't start eating something soon. I don't know how to handle them; teenage girls always scared the shit out of me even in school, and these are really scary – but they're so weak . . . ' Joseph throws up his hands to emphasise his incomprehension. 'See you afterwards for a kick around?'

Bruce sleeps fitfully. He knows something has happened with Jane – a door has opened a little way. He feels disturbed and angry. Something happened to her, something made her talk in that little girl voice and wallop that doll. Should he go on, looking, hoping, allowing her to lead him into her world? Can he bear to stand next to Jane in her world and witness what she's been through?

A sudden horror rises, as if from the foot of his bed, and rushes at him, unexpectedly. He sucks in the air sharply as the realisation hits him. She's in here because she murdered her children. She murdered a baby doll right in front of him – but the baby doll is her.

He gets up and paces about the room, makes himself a drink of hot milk and finds a trashy novel to read until he falls asleep, determined not to be invaded by his own fears of inadequacy and Jane's unstable inner world.

Fifteen

Where the brightness stops, the world ends – not with a bang, but a whimper, as T.S. Elliot says. And after the brightness, the dark: the space dark, the timeless interstellar spaces. Infinity. I will be where I will be, cradled in the moon's arms, asleep again; I will be back before time began.

Tonight I see the moon through the windows. The lunatic surveys *la lune, la lune est morte, comme tout le monde. Moi, je suis morte aussi.* Silent and dead, we view each other, the moon and I.

I cannot speak to them. They are concerned for me, I know that, but I have retreated, taken myself away from them all. I am locked up in three ways: in here, in my mind, and in my secret self. Dr Bruce cannot reach me here, though he still keeps trying.

And I feel no anger, and I feel no pain. Maybe I am dead, really dead. I am dead but walking. How can this be?

It's all grey now, all the faces, all the places, all the traces of faces. No colours, no warmth. I exist as a wraith, a shadow, a ghost.

'Jane!'

It's Elsie, good old Elsie. She calls me, but I cannot respond.

'Jane! You're not speaking? What's wrong?' She holds out her hand towards me. I see it but I don't take it. Elsie is grey and dead, and far away from me.

'Jane? Come on, look lively. It's shampoo night tonight.'

I shuffle along in front of Elsie to the shower, get out only when she tells me, keep still while she dries my hair. But I am dead. She doesn't persist.

Why am I living? Who for? For Dr Bruce? I saw him yesterday, but I couldn't speak to him.

I took the doll and held it. Then I wrapped it up and

put in it a box. Its eyes wouldn't shut, so I put sticky tape over its face. I put the box with the doll away in the corner, under a chair. It has gone.

Dr Bruce watched me closely and asked me questions. Is the doll baby dead? Is this a coffin box? How old are you now? I became angry with his questions and wanted to hit him, but he said he could see I was angry and didn't want to talk.

He asked at the end, what did I want to happen to the doll?

'Gone,' I said, in my little voice, and I pushed the air with my hand.

'You want me to take it?' he asked. I nodded.

So what would we do next?

He had a bag with things in it. I decided to do a drawing, a drawing of a tiny person, lost in a chaotic universe.

Sixteen

Bruce looks at his watch. Time to go and meet Jane. How should he be with her? She puzzles him.

He fetches the doll and his bag, with a few other things he thinks she might use, and walks thoughtfully along the corridor to the ward. He considers, as Ken unlocks the doors and studies his security pass, what it must be like to be locked up like this. Did these people never leave? Could they never be trusted to re-enter society? And how would anyone ever know they were well, if they never had an opportunity to test themselves out in the real world again?

Bruce is aware of the events that led most of the patients to be locked up, but as far as he is concerned those events happened in the past and he does not wish to concern himself with them now.

The staff think him inept and arrogant, though undoubtedly well-meaning.

Jane's file is open in the staff duty room, where Elsie is looking through it with a puzzled frown on her face. Bruce glances at her as he walks by, and Elsie looks up and registers his passage along the corridor.

'Stupid prat,' she thinks to herself. 'Thinks he can change things, when everyone knows patients like these are here for life, and I've never known anyone respond to treatment enough to be considered a hundred percent safe. Allowing them to hope that one day they can leave is pretty bloody stupid. It just lets them down and leads to more work for us. But these medics never look further than the ends of their noses. Research, huh? I'll research him if he comes in here afterwards.'

Seventeen

I'm lost again, trying to find a balance, a mode of being that is quiet and allows the voices to stop – that lets me get some rest. I sit in the posture, in the half lotus position with my palms uppermost, fingers gently curled. I imagine things falling into these hands: feathers, wisps of leaves, gauzy fabrics, snowflakes. It's quietening, soothing. I have retreated a long way inside now. The pink light in the room protects me, and I feel held, secure. I know Ken, or Marie – the new nurse who replaced Trevor – are watching me, but that's good, that's good. They care; they wouldn't let anything happen to me.

The invasion happens without warning. Dr Bruce looks into the room and calls my name. My head begins to fizz; anger and panic are at war with one another.

'DO NOT DISTURB DO NOT DISTURB DO NOT DISTURB!'

My voice comes from nowhere, screams at him, the words creating a barrier between us.

'Come and help me, someone! Leave me alone!'

Ken is there now too. He saw what happened. He reassures me, tells me Dr Bruce can come another time, but my ears are full of sealing wax, stopped up with anger. I arch my body forward and smash my forehead on the ground, again, again, again. Ken is there instantly. Someone is screaming. Is it me? Ken is holding me, and other staff have appeared to help him. They hold me as only they can, with firmness and containment, and I let them, I let them. No Dr Bruce today.

Losing It

Eighteen

Dr Bruce is appalled at what has happened; he cannot believe Jane is capable of such strength. The side of his face feels bruised where she let fly as they carried her back to the restraining room. He had been so sure she was okay with him, that the two of them had a good rapport. He only called her name for God's sake, they can't accuse him of having provoked her. He decides he'd better speak to Ken.

'Ken, can I have a word?' Ken nods his assent and holds the duty room door open for Bruce.

Elsie looks up. 'Is she all right?'

Ken nods. 'She'll be all right in a while. She doesn't like being disturbed when she's in that room. It's the only place where she seems to get some respite.'

He looks grave and Bruce knows he doesn't like him. 'I didn't realise. I'm sorry.'

'Well I did warn you about her. She's fine if you handle her right, but she hasn't been sleeping lately and when she's agitated she needs careful handling. She'll be okay.'

Ken turns his back on Bruce and the doctor realises he is going to be difficult to deal with.

'Ken, I'd like to try again.'

'What, now?'

'No – maybe tomorrow morning. Can you ask her? About ten o'clock?'

Ken turns round. 'Doctor, I don't agree with what you're doing with Jane. You and I know she'll never leave here. Our job is to let her live here as a patient as peacefully as we can, so that she doesn't harm herself or others. Anything that gets in the way of that is not to be welcomed.'

'But supposing, Ken, that we could work with someone like Jane and restore them to normal function – so they could live semi-independently, for example . . .?'

Elsie joins in. 'The world out there made Jane the way she is. Any of us would be crazy if we had been through what she has. Here she has sanctuary at least.'

'Thank you, Elsie. You're entitled to your opinion of course.'

'Maybe you should read her file.'

'Is that it there? Thanks.' Bruce takes the file with mock humility.

It is a life, made up of notes others have written, letters which will never be read, forgotten comments and judgements that no one will so much as glance at again, undeciphered prescriptions.

He holds it for a moment, recognising it for what it is.

Nineteen

Dr Bruce flicks through the file, his mind not really on it. Phrases rise from the page and lodge in his mind.

"Referred to Child Guidance 1966."

"Mr Pryor's imprisonment is having a damaging effect on the family. Mrs Pryor claims to find Jane and her sister hard to control."

"An underweight little girl, with some bruising to buttocks, and a skin rash, caused, mother says, by her incessant bed wetting. Mother claims the bruising follows a fall on the stairs."

"Health Visitor to visit again soon".

How old was she then? 1966 . . . she was only eight.

He flicks through again.

1979. Psychiatrist's Report. "Miss Pryor has apparently recently returned from Belgium, where she went to live with her common law partner, Mr Ducasse, by whom she has two children, Juliette and Christophe. I gather she left the children behind in Belgium with their father. Miss Pryor complains of having irrational impulses, associated with some suicidal ideation. I gather her relationship with the children's father was not a happy one and I put it to her that she may be suffering from an understandable reaction to leaving him and her children behind, as well as her mother's illness . . ."

Bruce is confused. Jane, Michelle, Juliette, Christophe, the doll – they're all mixed up in his head; maybe in Jane's head too. What has Jane been showing him?

Twenty

I'm back in the room again, the meditation room with the pink light and the cushions. They're watching me again. They must, of course they must, I understand that. Elsie is watching over me.

I close my eyes and sit in the posture, breathing quietly and deeply. No Dr Bruce today, I will not be disturbed. I am slipping back, slipping away, moving backwards in time. Henry gave me a tab of acid, I know what it is, but he told me it would make my mind better. Henry is cunning; the nurses don't know the half of it. He has stuff sent to him in teeny microdots under the stamps on his letters. It's on my tongue, and my mouth has gone numb. I breathe quietly. Let me be here, let me rest.

Losing It

Twenty-One

We went to Belgium on a motorbike, Fedo and me, when I was only sixteen. How long ago it seems now. I had never been out of England before. From Ostend we travelled south to the Ardennes, me three months pregnant.

I was sick at every petrol station and café we stopped at, and Fedo hit me when I cried and wanted to go home.

'Home to where?' he asked. 'You wanted to get away from them. You chose to come with me. Didn't you?'

He was right. I left behind a house so dirty and broken down that I was ashamed to let Fedo see it. My mother was drunk again on the morning I left. She was always drunk; she stank of it, of the cheap vodka she got from the merchant seaman who called to see her when his ship docked. The stains on her purple dressing gown made me recoil from her embraces, and her breath was sweet, like rum and pear drops. She used to feel sorry for herself at times and would want to embrace me, but she disgusted me.

So we travelled on, with my few clothes in the pannier and very little money, until we came to the river where the site was. We rode through the entrance gates at ten o'clock in the evening and the site manager greeted Fedo loudly. Finally we stopped and I got off the motorcycle, my legs sore and tired, burning my ankle on the exhaust as the bike tipped over. I remember the caravan well, going in there that first time. Fedo's things were there, but a mouse had been in the cupboards and the caravan smelled of musty leaves, damp paper and mouse droppings. There was a Belgian porn magazine on the floor, the pages yellowed, showing a girl bending over with her fanny open. I didn't want to look at it, but I couldn't look away. Fedo lit the gas and put a kettle of water on to boil. There was no electricity until the morning. The foam mattress we slept on was dirty and the cover torn, but I put up with it. Fedo didn't notice. He had sex with me as usual, roughly and quickly, not caring if anyone saw us through the caravan windows, which were dusty and had no curtains. I knew he'd sleep then and I would be safe. I lay beside him thinking about everything. I didn't want to think about the baby. I'd told Fedo, but he ignored me, saying it was my business. I think Juliette was his baby, but I will never be sure. How young I was! How little I knew about life!

Fedo's stubbled chin poked out of the blankets in the dull morning light. His dark glossy hair stuck out at angles where he had slept on it. Asleep, I could almost like him; he looked so vulnerable, and yet I knew the minute he opened his eyes I would once more be under his spell, in thrall to him, with his tattoos and his cruel, strong, muscular arms. I hated him for what I knew he would do, for the times when he'd hit me, for treating me like his possession – worse than his dog. Sometimes any attention is better than no attention at all, and God knows I had been used to that. The child within me stirred feebly, and I was cold, so I slid off the bed space and tried to find a match to light the gas. There were woodlice in the damp cupboards under the draining boards, and dried up teabags blocked the dirty brown sink. It would be my home for the next four years.

Fedo sent me out into the town that night, to find some trade, though I protested that I needed a day to recover. He did a deal with the man on the gate, Hubert, to get me customers, and in the car parks further along the river I took clients, seven or eight a night, and the van began to feel quite cosy with the money Fedo let me spend on it. He used the bike to do errands for Hubert during the day, so after I'd slept I sometimes had the place to myself.

Fedo. He was my protector and the one who hurt me, the one who needed me for sex, but would loan me to others for money – then hit me when I protested. My skinny belly, well hidden under my jacket, began to swell with the baby, but no one noticed in the dark until I was almost six months pregnant. Fedo told me to get rid of it. I told him it was impossible, so he went off to find someone who would do it for me, but he must have been unlucky because he came home in a terrible mood, shouting and swearing at me. I kept him at arm's length and managed to get out of the door and run to Hubert, and Hubert sorted it out with Fedo, telling him that if the police got involved they would all be losers. When I crept back later that night, Fedo was awake and hit me anyway, punching me in the stomach, in the hope I would lose the baby.

'You little slut!' he screamed. 'I told you to get rid of it. I don't even believe it's mine, you bitch. I'm not raising any bastard child of yours.'

'But it is yours,' I protested, writhing in pain, yet not fully believing it myself. 'I can't get rid of it, I'm too far gone. I'll probably lose it anyway now.'

I sobbed, unable to control the tears, and he flung me to one side.

'Bitch,' he repeated, searching my pockets for money. I should have left him then. But to go where? He had my money; I had nothing. Home was worse, if you can believe that. I massaged my bruised belly and checked that I wasn't bleeding. But Juliette was safe. Then.

Twenty-Two

My time in here is up. Elsie is padding along the corridor to fetch me.

'Jane.' Her voice is soft. 'Time to come back now.'

I sigh and gradually unwrap my arms and legs. I feel strange and my tongue won't work. Elsie doesn't mind. She waits for me to get up, quietly and patiently. I suddenly find myself crying, huge tears roll down my face and drip from my chin. Elsie is kind, but she doesn't know what to do. She would like to put an arm round me, but isn't sure how I'll take this. I stagger like a limping horse back to my room. She talks to me all the while, about nothing in particular, just everyday things about the other patients and her little dog, Rascal. She's shown me photos of Rascal before. I wish I could have a dog.

It's suppertime, and I sit with Thomas and Henry. Henry gives me one of his smiles. I want to kick his teeth in. He thinks I owe him something. Thomas is eating in a way that disgusts me, chewing his food and rolling it around at the front of his mouth, his big tongue like a pink slug, all wet and sticky. I shout at them to stop him doing it, but they don't, and they ask me if I would prefer to eat my dinner on another table.

I will not give in to them. I will not. So I leave the table and go without my supper. Later, Elsie comes and asks me if I want a game of Scrabble.

It's a strange game we play, Elsie and I, and the words we make have a strange significance. Trash. Empty. Daze. Winter. I let Elsie win.

Twenty-Three

The nurses are talking to one another, comparing notes. Robbie is writing his report about the incident with Thomas.

'Do you think Jane provokes Thomas?' he asks Elsie.

'It's hard to say. She doesn't like his table manners, but then neither do I. He knows what he's doing all right. He knows if he eats in a disgusting way it winds her up, and it doesn't take much to get her going. You know, she was in tears again today when I called her out of the quiet room. Any ideas what that's about?'

'Not a clue. I haven't had much to do with her lately. She won't speak to me, as you know.'

Robbie's forehead, usually creased horizontally, creases vertically as he talks to Elsie. He worries about the patients and his handling of them. Ken always appears so confident, Elsie so wise.

'She hardly speaks to me at the moment either,' Elsie replies. 'She used to say quite a lot. We played Scrabble tonight, but she only said four words during the whole game.'

'What were they?'

Elsie thinks for a moment. 'Trash, empty, daze and winter. Just some of the words on the board.'

Robbie thinks about the words, says them aloud to himself. 'Pretty much the words that describe some part of her?'

'They are pretty gloomy words, aren't they?' Elsie taps her biro on her teeth as she considers them.

'What do you think about her continuing to see Dr Townsend?' asks Robbie.

'I don't know. Sorry, that's a cop out. I suppose I haven't made my mind up yet. I think he's coming in tomorrow to discuss it.'

'As long as he gives us proper notice and we don't have to haul her out of the quiet room, like we did before . . .'

'Well. I won't be around to sort her out if it goes

pear-shaped again.'

'On leave?' Robbie enquires. Elsie nods. 'Going anywhere nice?'

'Bruges with a friend, on one of those cheap three-day deals, then I'm going to spend time sorting out the garden.'

'Have a good time. Are you knocking off now?' Elsie yawns and nods. She's very tired and just wants to go home and put her feet up for an hour before she starts packing. She trudges down the corridor to say goodnight to Jane.

Twenty-Four

Elsie comes to see me in my room. I'm reading *Black Beauty*. Elsie tells me she's going on holiday for a few days and that I must be nice to Claudia, who is starting work here tomorrow. She tells me Dr Townsend will come and see me tomorrow too if I want, and that they'll give me plenty of notice.

I nod. My tongue is dead. It won't work. I don't want to say anything.

Elsie tells me she's going to a town in Belgium called Bruges, with her friend, and that she might bring me back some Belgian chocolates. I start when she says Belgium and she notices.

'Jane, you look startled.'

'Belgium. You're going to Belgium.'

'Yes?' I don't reply and there's a long pause. 'Why?'

My tongue is thick in my mouth. 'My husband was Belgian. We lived there.'

'Oh? Whereabouts?'

'Further south than Bruges. At Dinant. We lived there . . .'

I can't go on. I feel something dark and awful inside me, growing, threatening to break loose and kill me.

Elsie looks closely at me. 'Jane? What's wrong?'

I throw myself off the chair and beat my fists on the floor, banging my head – up down up down – while Elsie calls for help. They come quickly and restrain me, Robbie gives me an injection to calm me down. Elsie is in tears. Finally she leaves.

Twenty-Five

"It's the end of the world as we know it, it's the end of the world as we know it, and I feel fine . . ."

I have been put on watch and I'm in bed, although it's early. The other residents are in the TV room with Ken. I don't like that room. The chairs have holes in the arms where Thomas tries to pluck the stuffing or whatever it is out of them. He picks away, pick pick pick. Pick pick, you make me sick. The TV is in an alcove in the wall, so no one can interfere with it. There's a sign on the door of the room that says "No patient must be left unattended in this room, for any reason".

Philip is not allowed in the room. He thinks the voices in his head come from the TV, and he gets confused by the other voices – the normal voices – that come from it. He goes mad and smashes things when the voices tell him to. The staff have told him that the voices have to stay in the room with the TV, and he sort of believes them. He's standing outside my room now, rocking backwards and forwards.

Robbie comes on watch.

'Come on, Philip, back to your end of the corridor.'

Philip laughs his insane laugh and rocks off down the corridor. He raps his fingers on my window as he passes. I hate Philip.

'All right, Jane?' I nod, tiredly. My head is bruised. My hands are sore. Robbie wanders away. There is a TV camera outside my room. They've switched it on. After last time they're not taking any chances.

Twenty-Six

On castle walls the daylight falls.

I am half asleep, and daylight is filtering through the window. We will have to get up soon, but I lie here, feeling content for once. It's a strange feeling. The drug they gave me last night must have been very powerful. I'm usually a great deal more agitated than this. Anyone will tell you that.

I shall go and have breakfast. Porridge and toast, I expect, but I feel hungry today and I'll eat anything. I used to make porridge for Juliette when she was a baby. I won't think about that.

The past is like a leaky dam. I can't stop the water leaking, and I can't deal with it when it does. Dr Bruce does not understand that if the dam broke I would drown for sure, so I live, or exist, in the false reality of now. But when the past rears its head like a tidal wave I have to hold it back at all costs. Sometimes it smashes into me, knocking me to the floor, so that I lose my bearings and myself. They know this here.

Suppose I go back to see Dr Bruce today? Too much has happened that can never be put right. I don't know if I want to go, I don't know if I can bear it.

Losing It

Twenty-Seven

"The psychiatric approach to the study of abnormal personalities has in the main been a clinical one and has not been made easy to follow by the use of the term psychopath. In general psychiatrists have tended to call psychopaths those patients with abnormal personalities but this is not universally so. The two concepts of psychopathy and personality disorder were most succinctly united by Schneider who defined psychopaths as those abnormal personalities who suffer from their abnormality or cause society to suffer.

... It recognises that someone can have an abnormal personality without being regarded in some way as ill or antisocial, i.e. distinguishes between "pathological" and "non pathological" personalities. This is important because the term "psychopath" has come to be regarded . . . almost as a term of abuse.

The striking feature of so many psychopaths is their remarkable degree of immaturity of personality development. They react to the whim of the moment in much the same way as does a small child who has tantrums if his wishes are not gratified immediately."

(Lecture notes on Psychiatry, James Willis, Blackwell Scientific Publications 1979)

Twenty-Eight

Bruce Townsend comes in mid-morning and speaks to Claudia and Ken about his proposal to continue working with Jane. They are non-committal. Claudia can't offer an opinion, having only just arrived. Experienced staff are a bit thin on the ground, Bruce thinks, having lost Trevor, and with Elsie being on leave. He might mention this to the ward manager. Then he decides against it. He's caused enough trouble as it is, and before long he'll be a marked man. Whistleblowers are dealt with viciously in this place and he's not about to rock the boat this time. Dr Khan, the consultant psychiatrist, is less than enthusiastic about the work Bruce wants to do. Trouble looms ahead, and if the staff complain about him making their life more difficult he will be in serious trouble. But he does want to work with Jane, wants to test out some of his theories about treatment, and she has responded. She has. The staff can say what they like, but he knows he cracked her armour, he got close to the real Jane, the child she'd once been. He goes back to her file for another look.

Twenty-Nine

Juliette was born in the hospital. Fedo was away fixing some deal, and a neighbour took me in. I always thought Juliette waited until it was safe to come out, that it was only possible for her to be born when Fedo was absent. He got back while I was still in the hospital and cursed when he didn't find me in the caravan. I think the neighbour told him where I was, but he didn't come to the hospital. The nurses were kind, and concerned about me going back to the site with a newborn babe, so they kept me in for eight days. I knew I would suffer when I got back for having been away so long. I looked at Juliette, so small, wrapped in her hospital blanket, and knew I had to do my best to look after her. But she was already like a doll to me. I could pick her up, put her down, leave her, come back to her, and there was nothing there. Do you understand me? It's important that you understand me.

Listen. Pay attention.

Juliette was my possession. Her cries didn't move me. Her little scrunched up features were those of a pinched doll. I fed her from a bottle, at arm's length, and made sure she didn't cry and upset Fedo. How did I do this? Well I had my ways of silencing her; I'm not saying what those were.

Perhaps I had post-natal depression. But I could never have admitted to it; it wasn't allowed; Fedo would not have tolerated it. So I went through the motions.
Fedo acted as though Juliette didn't exist. He took no interest in her.

'Put that thing down,' he would order me when I picked her up in his presence. He went out most nights to visit the prostitutes, but he resented having to do so.

Sex started again between us as soon as the bleeding stopped, and I was glad. It kept him away from me at other times and it was the one thing I could offer him that he seemed to want. I did not realise I was pregnant again until later, five months after Juliette was born.

When Juliette smiled at me for the first time,

hopefully and winningly, at seven weeks, her smile affected me. I wouldn't call it love, I don't know what that is, but without realising it I smiled back. Some days I saw her smiling as a trick, a ploy to get me to do things for her. I hated her then. Hadn't she had enough of me; she had been inside me for nine months, what more did she want? She had no right to expect more, did she?

Yet, from somewhere within me, I found the ability to care for her. I thought of my sister and her dolls, how she would put them to bed, tuck them up and give them drinks, while our mother lay sozzled downstairs and our father shouted and shook her. I used to watch. And when I wanted to play dolls, Michelle became my baby.

After our father went to prison it was different for a while. The shouting stopped, and at least we could sleep in our bed at night knowing that he wouldn't come. But in a way, though we hated him, we missed him too. Our mother didn't really change, and now she had no one. She hid from us and from the world, though I expect she tried to do her best.

The social workers used to call in to see us, and Michelle and I learned to shut up and say nothing. It was Michelle who told about my father, but she was only little, she couldn't help it.

When Fedo found out I was pregnant again he told me to get out. I begged and pleaded with him to let me stay. Where else could I go? What else could I do? I asked a neighbour to listen for Juliette when I went out on the game, and as long as I was working Fedo let me stay.

Some days in the caravan were peaceful. I washed the bedding and Juliette's clothes, swept and tidied, took her along the river in her pushchair. There were bloated dead fish, washed up at the edge of the banks. The long barges went past, carrying cement and wood, anthracite and animal feed, to Antwerp and back. I wished I could live on a barge, all cosy in the living quarters, able to move on, up or down the river, rocked by the water's lapping motion. I could almost feel love for Juliette at times like these, watching the river and the barges, holding her in my lap to look.

Thirty

Dr Bruce is here to see me. I have stayed here in my room after breakfast, writing stuff. They always want to know what I'm writing. There's no privacy here, even for your own thoughts. I write words, nonsense words, in any order. I know what they mean. Dr Bruce invites me to go into the interview room with him, and Robbie comes with us to wait outside.

Dr Bruce is kind today.

'Hello again, Jane. I'm sorry about the other day when I came to fetch you for our session. I didn't mean to interrupt you.'

I am startled. Doctors don't usually apologise. I look at him, take in what he's said.

He opens his bag, the one with the dolls in it. He takes out the doll I said was dead and puts it on the floor in its box, where I put it the last time we met.

'Last time we met, the doll was dead,' he reminds me.

I correct him. 'Gone,' I say.

He looks at me. 'Gone,' he repeats. Then, after a pause, 'Is gone the same as dead?'

I don't answer. How can I? Can things not really alive be dead?

I snatch the paper and pencils he has put out on the table. I draw a tiny scribble shape, almost tearing the paper. Then I make a big circle round and round and round, black, heavy, almost hiding the scribble shape. He tips his head on one side to look. He wants to say something but he's afraid it might be wrong. Go on, Dr Bruce, try.

'Jane, can you tell me what that is?'

I say nothing. My hand is still going round and round. I can't stop. He tries again. 'It's going round in circles. Something is trapped in the middle.' I nod. 'You?'

I rip up the paper, grab the pencil and stab the chair. Robbie moves to the door. I stop. The pencil is broken. Dr Bruce means well, but he goes too fast.

The session ends.

Thirty-One

I'm back in the quiet room.

Lunch was fine because Thomas was at the hospital being checked for something. Henry is okay at meal times; he eats normally.

I sit on the cushions and breathe deeply, slowly, allow myself to relax. Claudia is outside, but she's not staring at me. She seems all right, Claudia, but not the same as Elsie.

I close my eyes and see the barges once again, going up and down the River Meuse. Warmth, summer sunshine and insects are all around me, and I am on a barge, chugging down the river to Antwerp and the sea. The white gulls, which have abandoned the sea to live on this inland waterway, roost on the bridges and eat the enormous greeny-brown spiders that hide in the corners of railings along the embankments. I hear the sound of rifle shots again as the hunters in the woods go after their prey. In this land, nothing that moves is safe from the hunters. It's a place where meat is king.

Here on the barge I am safe. Floating, navigating weirs and locks, tying up for the night, the fish and the ducks all the company I need. The engine is like a heart beating in the depths of the hold.

Something invades; something is trying to intrude on this dream. A face, faces, in the water. Children's faces.

Come back, come back! You can't have that sort of dream, that sort of experience, in the quiet room. It's too close to the edge, too close to the centre, too close, too close.

I fling my arms wide and come out of the posture. I stand and go to Claudia, who is yawning outside. Where is my quiet sea, my calmness? I feel bereft. Dr Bruce has destroyed my fragile peace.

Thirty-Two

Dr Khan is going to see me today.

Poor Dr Bruce, he started something but he doesn't know how to carry on. It's not his fault; he's impatient for results. He likes his medical standpoint of diagnose, treat and cure. He doesn't understand that beyond a certain point, to go back into the past – which is where he takes me – is a self-destructive act. None of us here can live with what we've done, what we've had done to us, what we still do and might do again. We keep it far out there, curtained off from our lives. Yet I do find myself thinking about it all, and then memories leak through, the memories of things which exist outside the boundary, beyond the curtain. This is where the pain is, the madness, the psychotic core. Dr Khan will treat me like he treats all his patients, briskly and matter-of-factly – to the point of brusqueness. If I don't answer immediately he will ask Ken, and Ken will have to speak for me. This is how it is.

The doctor who saw me before used to ask "How are we today?" and I answered "How many of us are there?"

At that point I wasn't sure, you see. I couldn't be quite certain that I had done the things they said I'd done. It was another self, another time, another place.

When he asked this again, later, I wondered if he meant that I should know how he was. "We", after all, means "us here". How could I know how he was, unless he was – in some way I didn't understand – mixed up with me, an extension of my personality? Which he may have been. So I would say, "The bit of me that is here in this bit is tired and not sleeping. I don't know about anything else".

But he wasn't interested in examining the boundaries of my experience, or in examining his own. He was interested in my medication.

I saw a letter once, about me, with "To Whom it May Concern" written on the envelope. Who was there who was concerned? Did somebody who was concerned about me write the letter? I shall never know. I shall go to the meditation room, if they'll let me.

'Ken?'

'Yes, Jane.'

'Can I go to the quiet room for a bit?'

'Hang on, I'll get Claudia to go with you.'

He puts out a call and Claudia comes from the kitchen, where she has been tidying up with Henry. Not tidying the knives, of course, just the other bits and bobs.

Henry is not to be trusted, even in the kitchen. He is sly, he takes advantage, but they don't know this yet, because he's new. Claudia comes and directs Henry to go into the resident's lounge, where Robbie is watching over things. A new staff member has joined us, from an agency, called John. He's big and fat, with a black beard. I don't like him; I don't like the look of him. He smells of sweat and aftershave. I won't let him come near me. He's sitting next to Robbie, learning the ropes.

Claudia takes me down to the quiet room. I have to leave the door open, but it's okay, I can cope with that. I sit with my back to her on the soft cushion and cross my legs, my spine straight and my neck relaxed. It's good to feel in my own space again.

Thirty-Three

Water is flowing slowly, sluggishly, along the river; it's khaki coloured, thick with algae, like warm soup. The barges go on down to the lock to wait their turn, the taxi boats with day trippers go upstream, towards the upper reaches of the river, where the cliffs rise high out of the water and rocks, and tree roots meld together at the water's edge.

I drift with the mayflies on the warm, scummy river water, which is cleaner than the tap water here, smelling as it does of chlorine and chemicals.

River water, ah, the memories it brings back. The soft, fishy fragrance of live river water. I float, I drift, I glide with the current, slowly, slowly.

A child's face appears in the water; a little child's face. Is it Juliette? The face watches me, hopeful and smiling. Suddenly I feel tears on my own face – my tears. It's my face I'm looking at, my tears that are falling. There is no Juliette, she's gone, gone back into the water. I'm alone. The world is empty now of her presence – even I do not exist, not really. I am a shadow, a half person, not even the sum of all my parts.

I ask Claudia to take me back to the ward.

Losing It

Thirty-Four

I am sad all day long. The image of a child's face hovers in front of me like a ghost. Oh, I know it's not really there, in the sense that I can't reach out and touch it, but my eyes still see it, my mind perceives it. Have you ever lost somebody and then seen them walking along the street, sitting in a train, entering a shop? For a moment, you have re-created them in your mind, but it turns out to be someone like them; something about the shape of the head, the turn of the neck, the smile, reminds you irresistibly of them, and you stare until they turn and look towards you. Then you realise it is not the lost one after all, but a cruel trick, a shadow, a phantom created by your own mind, for your own comfort.

Was the face I saw Juliette's? I cannot say. It was many years ago that I . . . but I can't think that thought, can't allow the memory to filter through a chink in the armour. That way madness lies.

Can I not mourn her, then? As I secretly mourned the aborted one, the one I let go of at thirteen? Yes, I killed it, or allowed others to do so. Yes it was murder, in its way, and yes, I mourned that dead one, no bigger than a strawberry, which they scraped from my womb. Killing it makes no difference, you see, in a way it just makes the grieving harder to bear. My strawberry baby exists somewhere, and reproaches me with sad, sad eyes. One day I shall join her. I am slipping down, my thoughts have become unthreaded, a word salad.

Crazy lost a baby don't don't understand me try to understand me suffering, suffering languish linger long for cannot have refused no no too terrible too terrible to bear.

Thirty-Five

'What the hell's Jane doing? Go see to her John, will you?' Ken stares at the monitor.

'What if she won't let me near her? You know what she's like.'

'If she gives you any problems, press the alarm. Don't muck about – she's capable of being violent when she's upset. Just take it slow and calm. You'll be fine.'

'I'm on my way.' He walks quickly down the corridor, finding Jane in the dining area, like a frightened animal at bay.

'Jane, what's the matter? Come out from under the table.'

'FUCK OFF FUCK OFF FUCK OFF FUCK OFF. FUCK. OFF.'

'Take your hands off your ears, Jane, and listen. I know Ken can see us, but he can't hear what I'm saying . . .'

'FUCK OFF FUCK OFF.'

'So I'm going to say it – if you don't calm down and come out from under the table, quietly, I'm going to give you something to really shout about. I promise you won't like it.'

'FUCK OFF! KEN! ELSIE!'

'They can't hear you. Shut up, or you'll be sorry. Quiet. That's better.'

Footsteps come down the corridor.

'What's the problem, John? You appeared a bit agitated.'

'Foul-mouthed bitch. The language! I feel like washing her mouth out with soap.'

'It's not our business to punish patients, difficult though they may be.'

'Might teach one or two of them a lesson, though. In the Challenging Behaviours Unit we learned a trick or two about stopping their little games.'

'But this isn't the Challenging Behaviours Unit; these people are here for life. We have to try to help them live out their days in the best way they can. It isn't easy for any of us. If you can't hack it, I suggest you tell Robbie and we'll try to find a replacement. We've got a good reputation here – and we don't want any scandals.'

'Okay – just saying, that's all.'

'Jane, come out, please. Do you want to talk? Okay, you don't have to. Go back to your room for a while until lunch then. Dr Bruce is coming after dinner.'

Ah, Dr Bruce is coming is he? Fancy that! Doctor Brucie Wucie Townsend of no fixed abode. Well, we'll show him, won't we girls? We'll show him what it means to spend your life being fucked up by other people. FUCKED UP.

'Can I have some dinner now, Ken?'

'They haven't brought it up yet, Jane. It'll be here soon I expect. Coming?'

I scowl at the new one as I walk past.

Thirty-Six

Dinnertime. Henry sits opposite me today, while Thomas sits next to Ken at the other end.

Thomas isn't allowed to eat with anything he could use to hurt himself. We've got shepherd's pie today, with peas, and he shovels it up noisily into his mouth. Henry looks at me slyly to see if I'm going to make a fuss. He winks, but I look away. Ken tries to start a conversation about EastEnders in an attempt to distract my attention from Thomas. But I no longer care.

After lunch, I go into my room and brush my hair, inspect the dark circles under my eyes. The face in the mirror looks back at me. It isn't me; it really isn't me. I cannot own it, in any way at all. I go to where Dr Bruce sees me, in the small side ward. He's late. Robbie watches me from the office.

Thirty-Seven

'Hello, Jane. Are you ready to work with me today?'

I sit. I don't speak. I don't trust myself to speak. He opens the bag with the dolls and things in it and puts it on the floor so I can see inside. I look but I don't move. He waits, patient for once. I pick up a small doll and hold it to me, tightly. Something starts at the back of my throat, something I'm not in control of, a sound that takes me by surprise and leaves my mouth, filling the room with noise.

It's a howl. I listen to it as if it were not a part of me. But it is, it comes from my throat, my chest, my guts. Dr Bruce looks around anxiously. Robbie moves nearer the window to see what's going on. Nothing. I sit and let this howl escape from my body, clutching the doll to my belly. Is this what madness really is? Watching yourself doing things, making weird noises and not being able to stop?

Eventually Robbie can cope with it no longer. He comes in. 'Jane!'

Dr Townsend sits there, not knowing what to do, helpless.

'Jane! Stop that!'

Dr Bruce interrupts. 'It's okay, Nurse. She'll stop in a moment.'

'It's not okay, Doctor. She's disturbing the other patients. She's also disturbing me.'

I stop. The howl becomes a wail, the wail a whimper, the whimper a heavy, sobbing sigh. Silence.

Robbie carries on. 'Dr Khan's coming up to see her in about half an hour. He'll need to her to be a bit co-operative. I think the session should end now.'

Dr Bruce knows he's beaten. He shrugs, like a spoiled child. 'Have it your own way. I wash my hands of it.'

'Come back to the ward now, Jane.' I trot along, meekly, after him. It's what I did with Fedo after all.

Thirty-Eight

Dr Khan is seeing Philip when I get back to the main ward. Philip comes out grumbling, muttering obscenities under his breath. The words are racist obscenities. Dr Khan can hear them from where he is, but he pays no attention. Dr Khan can tell himself Philip's madness causes him to say such things, that it is a symptom of his illness. Perhaps it is, but I also know that he is somebody who would probably have been like that anyhow. Madness just gives people an excuse for saying all sorts of things out loud which would normally be kept to themselves.

"Poor chap", people think, "he really does feel persecuted". But there are always questions to be answered. Philip came here because he couldn't, or chose not to, control the fearful impulses that led him to attack people in the street. It was this lack of control that led him to miss out on prison, that and the muttering. Diminished responsibility again, you see. I hate him. Sane or mad, I hate him. At least I'm clear about that. He spits on the floor as he passes me.

Dr Khan calls my name. I walk, followed by Claudia and watched by Howard, into the side room.

'How are you feeling these days?' A novel start. He's never asked me that before. Must have been on a course.

'Some days are better than others.' A safe answer.

'Eating and sleeping alright?'

I don't know what to answer. What's the point? He doesn't know how things outside your control can torment you, come out of the night and make you so afraid you can't even scream. The evil dream of psychosis. He doesn't know how it feels never to escape from the thoughts, feelings and words that attack you day and night. And the memories – he has no idea at all about those. I nod, dumbly, unable to say anything more.

'How have the sessions with Dr Townsend been going?' Ah, the million dollar question. 'Are they helpful?' I fiddle with my fingers. I don't know what to say. 'We can stop if you don't like the sessions.' He waits for my response. 'Do you want to continue?'

I begin to rock, backwards and forwards. I can't stop. It's what I do when I can't answer a question. I want and I don't want. I nod my head.

'So you want to carry on? Shall I tell Dr Townsend?' I nod. 'Let's have a look at your medication.'

He looks at my sheet and asks if the tablets I'm on are working, looks to Claudia and Howard for confirmation. They nod. But they ask to speak to Dr Khan, after I've left.

Thirty-Nine

I can hear an argument going on in the staff room. Claudia shoos me away from the door.

I sit and pretend to read a magazine. The staples have been taken out, so it's hard to hold. All the time, I'm watching for Dr Bruce coming through the door – it's his voice I can hear through the walls.

I want and I don't want to listen to the argument. I do and I don't want to know who is the victor. All my life has been like this, you see, I've never known anything else. Do you think maybe it was me, that I contaminated the world around me, driving my mother to drink, my father to things I will not disclose, Fedo to beat me? I must have had some part in it surely?

If it were not for me, Dr Bruce would not be arguing with Ken and Howard. Dr Khan is with them, but I can't hear his voice. Dr Bruce is in there making his case on his own.

I sigh and move away from the door. Claudia nods at me encouragingly. She and I stroll down to the TV room to join Henry.

Forty

Dr Bruce is heartily sick of working in the unit. Obstructive staff, a difficult consultant, lack of belief in what he's doing, and no notion that what he is allowed to do is in any way helpful to his patients; all these factors have conspired to make him reckless and yet afraid.

Ken is saying in no uncertain terms that he feels the sessions with Jane should cease. From his perspective, it's making Jane less easy to manage and therefore less safe. He doesn't like what he's seen of the sessions; it frightened him, as it did Robbie, to glimpse the depths of Jane's despair and need. He knows they will never undo Jane's past, at best she can only learn to live with it, so even if Dr Bruce succeeds in restoring her to some semblance of normality, it will then make it all the harder for her to accept her imprisonment, and for them to manage it. Dr Khan is listening to Ken with interest, but he keeps his thoughts to himself.

Dr Bruce defends himself by pointing out that if no one attempts to treat those with severe personality disorders, progress can never be made in this field. He believes Jane has responded well to the sessions so far, and it's early days. Jane comes to them willingly, doesn't she?

He forgets – and Ken reminds him – that Jane has a history of compliance, punctuated by outbursts of extreme violence. He argues that she doesn't know what she's letting herself in for, that you can't put these patients in charge of their own treatment as they don't understand their condition enough to know what's good for them.

Ken stops speaking, remembering Jane's baby voice in the session he observed on the screen. Baby Jane, with a baby voice, saying "Jane's crying", as if talking about a doll, not herself. Could Bruce Townsend be right, could it be helpful to Jane to go back into her childhood?

Bruce answers Ken's doubts in the only way he can. 'Ken, Jane's behaviour veers between two extremes, wouldn't you agree?' Ken nods. 'Is she being her adult self, or acting like a child when she is having a tantrum or rocking or banging her head, etcetera? I think the work I am trying to do with her simply acknowledges her need to become childlike, but it makes it more explicit, gives it expression if you like. If she can understand this, maybe it will help her, and therefore staff, to deal with it better.'

Ken is not impressed, though he has to admit the shaky logic of the argument.

'The big word is "if",' he comes back. 'My question is, what happens then? What if she does gain some understanding of herself and her history? She's still here, locked up, isn't she? And anything that makes the work of my staff more difficult than it already is, is going to have repercussions, as you well know. We have other patients to consider.'

Dr Khan steps in at this point.

'Surely,' he says, 'when this was first discussed, these issues were thought about? As I understand it, the work Dr Townsend is attempting to do here is part of a research project. It is also part of Dr Townsend's training. I suggest we review the situation in two months and see whether Jane's behaviour is still giving rise to concern. She seemed quite docile today when I saw her.'

Ken is not happy with this but what can he do? He decides to keep an even more detailed log of ward events which involve Jane, and to pin Dr Khan down further.

'Can we arrange another date for a meeting, Dr Khan, before you go?'

Three disgruntled individuals leave the room. Howard remains neutral.

Forty-One

Bruce strides down the passage oblivious to the world around him. Jane is waiting for him. He doesn't even glance at her.

Making straight for the staff canteen, he spots Joe on a side table. He is moodily drumming his fingers on the tabletop alongside a plate containing the congealed remains of some too-red pasta sauce and curling fragments of pasta shells. Eaten without enjoyment and discarded without regret, Bruce thinks, easing himself into the chair opposite. Joe tries to look friendly, rubs his hand across his face, yawns, and gives Bruce a bleary look.

'Just got off duty?'

'Nope. Went to an all-nighter with some of the staff from Clifford House. Can't even remember getting home, but I suppose Valerie put me to bed. Someone did. I'm feeling the after effects now though. What have you been up to?'

'Just had a run in with the ward again, over the woman patient I'm seeing there.'

'Serious?'

'Don't know. Could be, I suppose. They won't try anything new, scared of their own shadows, most of them, or it's too much trouble to even consider it.'

'Aren't you being a bit hard on them? After all, they have to do the day to day stuff. It can't be easy, from what you've said. Anyway, I think you're getting too involved in the whole thing. My anorexics now, if I worried about them all the time I'd be heading for an early grave. We just try to keep them alive somehow, by hook or by crook, so that eventually they get the message they're worth saving. But sometimes they don't make it. What do you do in your spare time?'

'Apart from kick a ball around with you sometimes, there's the odd game of squash. Not much, I suppose.'

'Women figure at all? Only since you and Fran broke up you never mention anyone.'

'Oh, I've got friends – you know. But no one special,

if that's what you mean.'

     'Well, you know what they say – all work and no play . . .'

     'Spare me the lecture, Joe.'

     'Sorry. Coming outside for a smoke?'

Forty-Two

In another city, a woman named Michelle, who has been troubled for many years, takes her destiny into her own hands. Deeply depressed and all alone, she makes it, drunk, to the railway line, where she lies down and waits. The driver of the train which kills her will never recover from the shock.

News of this comes to Jane's ward on a damp Tuesday morning. It is agreed that the parish priest will be the one to break the news to Jane of her sister's death, as Michelle always retained a nominal interest in the Catholic Church. The staff wait with a heavy heart for the aftermath.

Jane senses at once that this is not a social visit, and the priest wastes no time in breaking the news that Michelle has ended her life. He adds that it was a quick and sudden end – he doesn't say "painless", and that she will be missed by many people on the estate. He stresses that she must not be blamed for her actions; she was deeply troubled and unable to think clearly. He can't think what more to say, so waits for Jane's response.

Jane's mouth falls open as though she wants to say something, and she mouths his words silently to herself. She looks grey and crumpled, all the spark gone from her, and Robbie feels a surge of pity. What could she possibly have to look forward to, with the last remaining member of her family gone? She has nothing now, not even hope, no links to the outside world to sustain her, nothing, zero, zilch. Despondently, he leads her back to the ward.

Forty-Three

Heavily sedated, Jane withdraws from the world, but her mind gradually registers the news. This was her little sister, the one she tried to protect, the one she held next to her body for warmth in the wet bed when their father . . . she can't deal with that part of it.

She's left with feelings of having failed Michelle in some way. She last saw her a year ago when she came on a visit, but it isn't the gaunt, chain-smoking woman she remembers, hanging on between appointments with the psychiatrist and the CPN. It isn't the Michelle who had nothing to say to Jane – to the fucked-up sister who caused the family so much unwelcome publicity all those years ago. Or the Michelle who never forgave Jane for leaving her, though at the time of her departure to Belgium with Fedo, Michelle was in care and acting as if she hated the whole world.

It is the little girl Jane remembers, those walks in the park and the tiptoeing back in, hoping their mother would be still alive. The days when they clung together when there was no one else to cling to, when Michelle had been Jane's baby sister, tucking her dollies up in bed while Jane watched. Jane was not old enough to be a mother to her sister, and her mother not sober or adult enough to be a parent to either of them for long.

Jane knows sisters like her and Michelle are ten a penny. What are they worth, after all? As long as they're quiet and obey the rules and don't cost the taxpayer too much then everyone can forget about them. The state will look after them, won't it? But why should the state help a feckless drunken woman and her psychotic, child-murdering sibling? Jane knows that the world will see her family as plain evil – feckless at best. And she thinks that the world should be made to squirm.

Forty-Four

The day of the funeral is bright and clear, early May. Jane is allowed to wear a dark dress and jacket which Claudia brings in for her, being much the same size, and outdoor shoes. A decision is taken to drive Jane to the funeral, with Claudia to escort her and John for backup. What could happen in a crematorium miles from the main road, up a drive flanked by rhododendron bushes and pine trees, on a sunny spring day? There will be few other mourners, no one to upset, no one wanting photos.

The drive is a long one, around three hours, and they slip into the back of the chapel just as the priest begins the service. John stays in the car, listening to the radio. Jane, in a dress which doesn't belong to her, stares around, unsure of herself.

She has had few outings in her years on the ward. Only when she needs attention to her teeth, or medical treatment not available on site, is she able to leave the ward, closely accompanied by another. She feels unprotected away from the unit. Even in the chapel she feels exposed, and she stares at her feet. The priest, recognising her, allows them to remain in the seats at the back.

There are other mourners present – women from the estate who knew Michelle, a couple of drinking mates, the two children and their partners. These two whisper and point to Jane, but don't greet her. Natalie, the girl, skinny in black leather, high as a kite and hysterical, clutches her partner; Rick stands facing the priest as if something is about to be dispensed, his gaunt cheeks and hungry look telling of a heroin habit reaching its limit. His earring sparkles in the light which falls through the slanting window, and he grasps Natalie's hand as he remembers his father's funeral when he was two years younger – before it all needed blotting out so frequently. Perhaps there is something to be gained from Michelle's death, perhaps not. Natalie's tears might be real tears of sorrow for her mother, or they may be tears of pity for herself, trapped in a grey and desperate world without a parent to make amends to.

The service starts.

Jane's head, her dark hair swinging loosely around her face, is bowed in concentration as the priest intones the words of the service. She is being watched; she knows it. Twisting her fingers, she notices the paleness of her nail beds, the way her nails, cut every week by Elsie or Claudia, form neat half moons, white and clean. The hands of someone never allowed to wash up, or peel potatoes, or handle earth. Soft skin, pale pink, on her palms. Jane peers at her palms. The lifelines are indistinct at the top, where they join the roots of her fingers. Where does her lifeline end? She tries to trace it.

The priest's words come through, like tennis balls over a net, and she tries to bat them away. Claudia nudges her. She sits up and listens.

The priest, who knew Michelle only slightly, finally reaches the end of the service. The eulogy is brief, there isn't much to say. Michelle had a difficult life, had been unhappy in recent times, and who were we to judge her? She had been a support and friend to several people on the estate and he hopes those people present will find it in their hearts to comfort the relatives of the dead person.

'Ashes to ashes, dust to dust.'

The mourners stand in silence as the coffin is swallowed up by the curtains, as it makes its final exit. There are no encores.

Suddenly Jane throws her head back and snorts. A terrible scream begins to emerge from her, unbidden. Claudia stands up and holds Jane's arm. Quickly she hustles her from the chapel, but the scream increases to an ear-splitting banshee shriek. Then Jane runs, Claudia at her heels, cursing John, who is asleep in the car on the other side of the crematorium, his ears filled with Test Match Special. A track plays from a tape Michelle had left in the machine on the day she died, as the other mourners, perplexed and alarmed, walk stiffly and warily towards the daylight.

Jane runs across the lawns, past the rhododendron bushes, avoiding the driveway, heading for the boundary – a wire fence with rose bushes trained against it – and beyond it open country, rough pasture, trees and parkland. Jane runs surprisingly swiftly, and Claudia regrets the chips they ate on the journey, and the cigarette which followed them. Claudia has abandoned her usual uniform and her skirt is not made for running in, but then neither is Jane's.

Suddenly, Claudia catches her foot in a half-excavated rabbit hole and falls full-length, stinging her hands on pine needles and rabbit droppings. Jane, now silent, races on, arms outstretched, as if running to meet a lover. She reaches the boundary fence, straddles it with a hitch of her skirt, and leaps away through the coarse grass down towards the woods. Soon she is out of sight.

Claudia stands at the boundary fence, bent over, trying to get her breath. She tells herself it's no good going after her. She won't go far. The priest and several interested observers gather at the boundary.

'I'll go and get the car,' Claudia says, anxious to get away from their curious eyes. 'We'll drive round to the bottom and pick her up.'

John comes lumbering over the hill at that point, having been woken by a member of the congregation. Claudia joins him thankfully.

'I knew this was a bad idea,' John says as they get into the car. 'People like her can't be trusted. Should never have let her come.'

'Oh I don't know. I know they're supposed to be locked up, but Jane's really only a danger to herself these days. It seems a bit cruel not to let her come when it's her only relative. I gather that Michelle used to visit her, and it's almost the only outside contact she had. She just needed to get away by herself for a while, I guess. We'll go right here, that should take us near enough to the bottom of the park. Can you see her anywhere?'

'We'd better radio base and tell them what's happened.

I'm supposed to be on duty this evening – damn, this would have to happen. You know she got me in the shit before?'

'Did she? How was that?'

'Oh, the other day she wouldn't come out from under the table. I dared to challenge her and got a telling off from Ken, would you believe.'

'Yeah, I heard about that. Ken's quite strict, does things by the book.'

'Well he's been on that ward too long if you ask me. He should try looking at how they do things in other units, that might loosen him up. Pompous prick.'

'Ken's all right. No sign of Jane. What do we do now?'

'I am not going out scouring the woods for her, that's for sure.'

'I suppose that means I'll have to go and look for her. Thank you very much.'

Claudia opened the car door and reluctantly got out.

Forty-Five

Under the May tree, in the long grass which quivers with small green creeping things, Jane lies, motionless. Her eyes are wide, noting every flutter of leaf, every flower edge tipped aside by industrious bees, every wisp of cloud tissue blown on the melting sky. Around her and above her, the green leaf-studded whorls of the woodland offer their silent, neutral voices to her. Jane, starved for so long of real contact with earth and sky, is dazed by the wonder of it all. Claudia is calling her name, but she stays so still, hidden in her grassy hollow under the May tree, that Claudia passes by and eventually goes back to the car to radio for help.

Forty-Six

People are hunting for Jane. It's dark, and Jane is long gone, hitching down the road to Dover, but Claudia and John have now been joined by the local police, who are half-heartedly trying to find her.

The helicopter, with its heat-detecting equipment, fails to locate any bodies hidden in the woods. She's gone; they finally accept that, and Claudia and John set out for the hospital again with heavy hearts, feeling they've failed, anxious about the possible repercussions.

Elsie has returned from her holiday and finds it hard to understand how Jane managed to escape. She tries not to be critical of her colleagues, but she knows Jane better than any of them, and she's worried she'll enter one of her strange trance-like states where she talks to no one and wanders around aimlessly until someone confronts her. Then, watch out world. She shoos Philip away from the kitchen, where he is loitering, cracking his knucklebones and grinning his grin. He lopes off. The other residents know something's happened, and refer to Jane's absence slyly as they eat her portion of food and sit in the chair she normally occupies. Thomas, strangely, seems upset that Jane is not around, testing staff patience to its limit by repeatedly chanting "Where's Jane? Where's Jane? Where's Jane?".

'Thomas, I told you, Jane's not here. She went to her sister's funeral and she got very upset and went for a walk. She'll be back again soon, you wait and see.'

'Where's Jane? Where's Jane?'

'Jane's gone.' It's Robbie, sick of the questions. 'Go and get ready for bed now, Thomas.'

'Where's Jane?'

But they won't answer him any longer and he goes to the changing area, repeatedly muttering "Where's Jane?" under his breath. He experiments with the sounds, extending the "where's" and snapping out the "Jane", then snapping out both together until it sounds like "whisjen", over and over, like a train vanishing into a tunnel. Finally he shuts up.

Elsie goes to the record files and draws out Jane's folder. Ken and Robbie are in a meeting with Claudia, John and the manager of the ward. Each of them is trying to offer a reason why this happened; a reason which may exonerate them and pass the blame to someone else. Luckily Jane has no relatives to sue or to make nuisances of themselves, but the papers may get hold of it and then there'll be hell to pay.

"Child Killer on the Loose", will run the headlines, "Psycho on the Run – mothers warned to keep their children close by them until brutal child murderer, Jane Pryor, is safely back behind bars".

Claudia and John talk about understaffing; Claudia is on a temporary contract and John is an agency nurse. Neither have had proper training in dealing with patients whose inner worlds are so chaotic, people who are so unpredictable, so primitive in their responses.

It's not fair to blame them, they argue, it could have happened to anyone. A team decision was made allowing Jane to go. Ken feels bad because he sanctioned Jane's special leave, and thought that Claudia and John would cope. The manager looks from one to another, unsmiling, and requests a full report. Something will go in their records.

Elsie, looking through Jane's file, is reminded again that Jane once lived in Belgium, and she thumbs through the early records until she finds a photocopy of a document sent on request by the hospital where Juliette was born. It's based in Dinant, in the Ardennes.

Elsie has a hunch, but knows it'll be scoffed at, and decides to wait until either Jane comes up for air and is caught and brought back, or the team become desperate in their attempts to find her.

Forty-Seven

No one thinks to tell Dr Bruce that his most problematic patient is missing, absent without leave, until he pops his head round the door of the duty room two days later.

Ken is on the phone to the police, who are informing him that there has been a sighting on the Dover to Ostend ferry. Ken is repeating himself. No, she had no money on her. No, no passport either. Just the clothes she stood up in, plus a small bag with tissues and tablets etc. Yes, of course they would inform the police if they heard anything.

Bruce listens with growing amazement and concern. Jane has escaped! How has this happened?

Ken is curt. 'She'll be brought back soon' he says, briefly relating the facts, unwilling to expand on them.

Guessing that this is not a good moment to arrange further meetings, or to annoy the staff when clearly they are feeling raw from whatever dressing down they have received from on high, Bruce makes a tactical decision to withdraw.

There goes my research project, he thinks, and he despondently makes his way back up to Ward 18 and the geriatric patients he is supposed to be working with this week. They've had their day, he feels; they don't need him. Most of them don't know when he's there with them. Unlike Jane. He feels guilty for having such unprofessional thoughts about his patients. He'll do his best by them, he always has, but his heart isn't in it.

Forty-Eight

Elsie waits several days before sharing her hunch with Ken and Howard.

'Can I talk to you both for a minute?' They look up, surprised. 'I have an idea about where Jane might have headed for.'

Ken and Howard raise their eyebrows in unison and Elsie continues. 'Do you remember the last bad do she had? Just before I went on leave?' They nod. 'That was because I told her I was going to Belgium. She used to live there, she said, down near Dinant. Her husband was Belgian.'

'They never found the guy, you know,' says Ken. 'He never came forward after her arrest. I've been reading the cuttings, he scarpered after they found the children and I don't think the police ever caught him. He was wanted on all sorts of other minor charges: pimping, drug dealing, receiving – the usual. So you think she may have gone back to the scene of the crime do you? Intriguing thought.'

Elsie nods. 'It's probably a crazy idea, Ken, but I think I know her better than anyone here. Can I go and look for her? I'll take it as annual leave if you like.'

'You're serious? You've only just got back, Elsie. I suppose I can't stop you if you insist on taking some . . . compassionate leave, but you'll have to keep it quiet, unless you find her of course.'

'I'll keep in close contact, I promise. Look, I'm retiring in November, I'd like to finish my time here usefully. I just have a really strong feeling that she'll have headed back there, sort of connecting up, if that makes sense.'

'Well what have we got to lose? You'll need help if you find her.'

'I speak passable French, and I'll get in touch with the local hospital if I find her, don't worry.'

'You're a brave woman, Elsie.'

Elsie smiles. She has earned the respect of Howard

and Ken over the years, and it's a good feeling. Smiling to herself, she sits down to study Jane's file. She puts on her reading glasses, gets a fresh notepad out of the drawer in the duty room and settles down to her task.

Forty-Nine

The rattling train skirts along the river valley, snaking around the bends under the wooded cliffs. It's not familiar, not from this angle.

I open my stolen bag and look at the passport photo; it certainly isn't me, but no one has challenged me – yet.

Stealing is easy. One visit to the toilet in the terminal, a wait for a woman to place her handbag on the floor while she sorts herself out, and I'm away with her bag before she's even aware of what has happened. I learned to survive by any means before I came here, and I haven't forgotten the lessons.

The countryside hasn't changed that much since I lived here. It's very green, spring is far advanced, and the river is flowing freely, topped up with fresh rain. Ducks scoot away across the water as the train passes. I remember this time of the year; the ducks were always fighting.

I feel very light and insubstantial, as if you could see right through me, as if I really exist somewhere else. I am in between here and there, in a limbo of my own choosing, and I've let go of the safety of my life on the ward. Elsie, Ken and the others are already fading in my memory, like wraiths, and yet I do not feel as if I can exist without them. But here I am. I haven't taken my tablets since I ran away and my mind feels as if someone is squeezing it, then letting go, as my eyes focus and unfocus, and my concentration becomes acute, then slackens again. Perhaps it will settle down. At present I don't care. In forty minutes I will have to leave the train and walk back along the track by the river, over the footbridge by the weir and along the other side, right out of the town until at last I come to the entrance to the site. Maybe Hubert will still be there, locked in his van, playing cards and drinking schnapps with his friends. Maybe not.

Fifty

Bruce is restless in his rented flat. He thinks of Jane and the frustration and anger that seem to surround her, how she draws people in with her helplessness and need, and how, in her moments of lucidity, she seems capable of being helped.

An image of his mother, long dead, comes to his mind, unbidden, begging him not to hurt her. Cowering in her bedroom, she had sealed up the windows and blocked the flue with thick wads of paper stuck with post office tape. Still she was sure "they" would come in and get her. Wild-eyed, she stared at her only son and did not know him. His twelve-year-old body had squirmed at her helplessness and the conflicting need to be with her and to leave. It was to this frozen tableau that his father returned – Bruce's mother dishevelled and rambling, embarrassingly half-naked in the corner of the room, and Bruce himself, half in and half out of the room, afraid to leave and even more afraid to stay, his school bag still draped over his shoulder, face screwed in a worried frown. He was so glad, so glad, that his father had come home.

His father took one look at his mother and phoned her doctor. Once again Bruce had witnessed his mother being led away from the house to the hospital, where she remained for twelve weeks, returning eventually, quiet and contrite, wringing her poor little hands and scuttling into the back room if anyone came to the door. Bruce loved and hated her. His father decided to send him to boarding school before hate took the upper hand, and paid for someone to come in on a daily basis, ostensibly to clean, but in reality to keep a check on his wife.

Although he was freed from the burden of worry about his mother, it took Bruce a good while to relax enough to enjoy his boarding school. It was the lesser of two evils, and his parents tried to make it easy for him, but he never invited friends home in case his mother was having "one of her do's".

It was when he was nineteen and at university that she had simply walked out of the house. She was found in the river two days later, washed up with sodden debris on the bank, sticks of straw and baler twine wrapped around her white, puckered legs. Foul play was not suspected.

Bruce tried to hide the fact that he was relieved as well as dismayed by her death. His father, ever a stoic, displayed little emotion and did not expect his son to do so.

Later, in the midst of his medical training, he was aware that the body of the small, pale woman on whom he was conducting an autopsy was very like that of his mother, and suddenly he was unable to bear the suffering she had been through, and that he had been through with her. He broke down and wept and had to be ushered out into the staff room and later sent home. He felt as though something in his head, which had been getting tighter and tighter through the years, had finally broken. Everything was unravelling at a speed he couldn't cope with. He managed to hide this from the other interns and took some time off to recover. The stigma of mental instability or illness terrified him. His whole future career would depend on hiding the extreme end of his emotions, whatever they were. He found solace in treating others and shut his unhappiness away somewhere. His partner, Fran, had almost released him from his self-imposed prison, but his terror of her becoming like his mother got in the way of her efforts to help him, and he shut her out, as he had his mother, unable to bear her closeness.

Now Jane is missing, and his mother's death has come back to haunt him once again. He finds himself ill at ease, unable to relax. Surely the past has gone? Why should it trouble him now? He had no part in his mother's death, felt only slight guilt about her treatment; his father had been a kindly if impatient man, unable to fully comprehend the extent of his wife's suffering. But somewhere, Bruce has a memory of his mother's love for him, a memory once obscured by her anxiety and terror about the world "out there", and what it might to do them.

Dr Bruce, thirty-three and single, now sits on his double bed where only one person sleeps, and marvels at the squalor of the room. The duvet needs washing, socks and underwear form an untidy pile in the corner, and his shelves are smeared in sticky coffee rings and clutter he has been too weary to put away: a postcard from a college friend, aftershave, an odd-shaped vase that Fran had made him in her evening class, a piece of driftwood from his last holiday with her, before she told him she was leaving him. He surveys these mementoes listlessly and goes to take a shower before leaving for work. He tries to avoid the kitchen, where a mound of take-away cartons wait to be thrown away. But the bin is full. He lacks any energy or enthusiasm to deal with the mess. Life has become rather empty, he reflects, and Joe's words hit home, uncomfortably near the truth.

Fifty-One

Dinant station looks the same; there's nothing here, it's only a setting down point. I have been set down, with my little handbag and my funeral dress, on this warm day in the Ardennes. It's further to the footbridge than I imagined, and I pass the riverside houses where housewives are pegging out their washing and feeding their rabbits. I keep on walking, breathing in the sounds and sights of spring, the swallows, seagulls and green rushes where the ducks are hiding with their babies. The river smells cold and fresh.

The footbridge is gleaming down near the bend, and beyond it I can see the trees of the campsite. The site we lived on is further still.

I should feel nervous approaching the last stretch of road. The campsite is already busy, and there's a new cabin and shower unit I don't remember. Not much else has changed. On round the bend – ha! That's funny.

Wait.

What has happened here? The gates hang on their hinges, blackened with rust. Hubert's shack at the gatehouse has gone, just a concrete plinth covered in litter and rubble. Where are the tidy vans, resting on their breeze block footings? Where are the cabins and sheds? There's a post with a letter box still attached, open and peeling. No letters for them today. Rubble everywhere. Why am I smiling? I am faint with hunger. Hun. Ger.

My feet stumble over gritty fragments of stone and breeze block. Soiled, smeared strips of newspaper rise and sink in the light wind near the river's edge, where the fishermen have squatted. It smells; the salty-sweet, shit smell of the riverbank.

My eyes focus on the only building left upright – the beer shack. The signs for Les Diables and Jupiter beer lean over as if already drunk. The shack is tilting; the umbrella stands where Juliette and I sheltered from the sun, sipping Fanta on summer days, are rusted and broken. Clematis has entered the windows, uninvited, curling green fingers around the empty shelves. Is there nothing left? I look round.

Away up the slope, where stacks of panelling from dismantled homes crowd out the green invasion, children are watching me. Gypsy children, I see at once. Nimble, suspicious and thin, they flit between the trees and the derelict shacks at the top of the site.

Walnut trees, plums and roses are growing untended. There is sadness in the air. What happened here? Why did everyone leave? Memories crowd in, but the past has gone. Here is a discarded mattress, its springs protruding like entrails from a gut.

Where was our caravan?

About

here.

I search the rubbish with my eyes, sift it, scour it, try to connect with something, carve an oozing scarlet tear in my leg where a splintered wooden stick strikes me like a snake as I walk. The standing blocks are still here, but there's no trace of the van. The children have taken the scrap for firewood.

Ah. Here's a shred of something I recognise. Lino, from the floor. Mottled brown and ochre. I pick it up, smell it, turn it over. It is thin and acid and the underside is damp, with a woodlouse sticking to it. But this was my home, where Christophe was born, where I lived with Fedo and Juliette, in fear and freedom. Nothing is simple; nothing is easy. Leaving or staying; being destitute with children to support, or being single, but missing them. Living or dying; it's all one in the end.

The lino goes in my pocket, one small piece of it. There's room for it. It is a symbol, a talisman.

Something is not connecting yet. I am here. The memories are clear and fresh, but something is not connected. What do I need to do now? Yesterday morning I was at my sister's funeral. Now I'm here. Maybe they're looking for me. Maybe not.

The standpipes still work, after wrenching and tugging, the water flows into my open mouth and spills down my chin. I wash my face with my hands and mop it with the tissues Claudia gave me so that I could weep for Michelle.

I can't weep for Michelle. She's gone. She chose to go. And succeeded.

In the end I couldn't protect her, or myself. Or the children.

Fifty-Two

A small three-year-old girl, with straight dark hair, wellington boots and wary eyes, pushed her toddler brother in his pushchair around the wet grass. The baby was fretful and had a cold. His nose was running and she wiped it briskly. He cried.

Their young mother came from her caravan, slim in her tracksuit, her hair tied up in a ponytail, her eyes hollow and tired. Grabbing the pushchair from the little girl she walked them both quickly towards the site entrance.

Asleep in the caravan, Fedo stretched on the bed, hitting the cupboard doors with his feet. He became conscious. She hadn't made his coffee. Where was she, the bitch? The brats weren't here either. Not that they dared to make a sound while he was in bed, but somehow it was strangely quiet.

He got up and searched for his jeans, which were under the table at the front of the van where he had kicked them off last night. He put them on quickly, finding enjoyment in fingering and clasping the brass-buckled belt coiled at the waist. He heard the swish and swipe of it in his mind, like a promise. Something he could call upon if needed.

He tugged on his black T-shirt and looked at himself in the washhouse mirror. Muscular, wiry, strong, he thought. Brown eyes fixed on his, challengingly. His chin, with its small dense goatee, thrust forward, daring the onlooker to respond. Hard, yes, he looked hard. It was how he liked it. No one messes with me, he thought, especially not that bitch.

He went to the tiny compartment the children slept in and searched it again, turning the mattress over and emptying the drawer before taking it out. The money had been taped to the underside before, where she'd hoped it would be safe from his prying eyes. He had found it, though; Juliette had given the game away.

The kid had to tell me, he thought, I would have

killed her mother. She knows she has to give the money to me. Stupid bitch. Where has she got to? He felt vicious.

The site was empty. It was early morning and no one was about; only a stray dog ambled past, pausing to piss on the back wheel of the bike. Fedo rushed out, enraged, but the dog had scampered off.

Jane sat in the café in the town centre and tried to imagine what she might do to them. Her body ached where he had hit her; she couldn't blame Juliette, the beating stopped when he found the money. How could she go on? Life was impossible.

The children sipped their drinks listlessly and watched Jane. They were all very tired. Juliette's long eyelashes lifted as she looked at her mother.

In French she asked, 'Where are we going, Maman?'

'I don't know. I'm thinking.'

'Are we going back to the van?'

'Don't ask me questions, Juliette. I don't know.'

'Cos I've left my Barbie there . . .'

Jane swiped her daughter's little arm, in its grubby pink sleeve, as it reached out to her.

'Don't ask questions . . . '

Juliette sucked in her breath sharply. Fedo, her mother; sometimes they were both the same.

She left the table and wandered to the river's edge, where she twisted and turned on the railings. Christophe had fallen asleep. It was a trick he'd learned.

Jane walked them home again later. Fedo had gone out.

Fifty-Three

Elsie wishes she hadn't suggested this trip. It was rash of her, and she regrets it.

She had some ideas about where Jane might be, having phoned the hospital in Dinant to ask for records of births. It had taken a while to find the information, but someone she spoke to remembered the case and was interested in the fact that Elsie was now searching for Jane. There seemed to be no one else interested in being involved in a search, but the psychiatric unit promised help if a direct request was made. It might be enough.

Alighting at Dinant, Elsie is struck by the thought that Jane, who has had several days start on her, might no longer be here, might be dead, or might not even have been here at all. There was a sighting on the ferry, but the guard at the train station is unhelpful and shrugs when shown Jane's photograph. No one is interested.

It is evening, and Elsie decides to book into the cheapest hotel she can find, have a bath and a meal and make a plan of action.

The hotel is near the castle ramparts, and she is given a grey little room in the eaves. It overlooks the square. Later, as she sits in a café off the square, dipping her chips in mayonnaise while waiting for the main course to arrive, she wonders whether Jane has been eating, and if so, what.

In the morning she will ask a taxi to take her to the Campsite au Pruniers, Jane's last known address. She was warned by the hospital that the site is no longer occupied, but she has to start somewhere, and this seems hopeful.

The rest of the meal arrives, and Elsie temporarily forgets about Jane and settles down to enjoy her food. She yawns. She is getting too old to be dashing abroad at a moment's notice. She stabs the mayonnaise with another chip.

The next morning, Elsie feels refreshed. Having

breakfasted on brioche and coffee, she finds a taxi to take her to the caravan site.

The river gleams silver in the morning light, gulls chase around the sky aimlessly. Elsie realises the taxi has stopped. Surely this can't be the place? But the broken sign dangling from the plum tree reads Campsite au Pruniers. She gets out and pays the driver.

It is a sorry place. Dilapidated, dishevelled shacks are all that remain. Elsie can see the remnants of hard standing where vans once were, several broken-down ones are left, gaping open, floors tilting crazily at the sky. No one is about. Could Jane be here, hidden in this landscape somewhere? There is no one to ask, no one to speak to.

The movement of a small body, flitting backwards and forwards up the slope between bush and burnt out car, flickers in the corner of her eye. There it is again. She picks her way over the debris towards it.

Fifty-Four

Christophe, the small, solemn toddler son of Jane and Fedo, cried for his mother. She was out with her clients and the neighbour who listened out for the children was asleep; only Juliette, his four-year-old sister, was there with him. Fedo would be back later.

Juliette unwrapped Christophe from his baby-smelling blanket and felt his nappy. He was wet and miserable. The girl's white T-shirt, which she wore in bed, emphasised her smallness and, unable to lift him, she rolled him over and tried to dry him.

The bedroom was a mess. Fedo had ripped out all the drawers looking for Jane's money and no one had put them back.

Christophe stopped crying and wanted to play. Juliette slapped him, urged him to keep still while she put a nappy on him. Where was their mother?

Juliette, the baby-girl, mother-sister, with knowing eyes and watchful face, tiptoed about the caravan, shivering slightly with the damp from the river. She found some biscuits and gave one to Christophe. Loneliness enveloped them both like a cloak. In the distance, Juliette heard the roar of a motorcycle engine and knew that Fedo was coming home at last. She got into bed and held Christophe tightly under the covers.

Fifty-Five

Days and weeks have gone by since yesterday.

It is all real. All the things from that time.

I hold the piece of lino in my hand and the smell brings back all the details of that caravan, the cramped living quarters, the children having nowhere to play indoors. The way Fedo took over the living area when he was there. The way he treated us.

He was angry at Juliette's birth, indifferent to Christophe's. He acted as though the children didn't exist; to him they were things, inconvenient things who had no right to feel hunger or pain. I went along with that when he was there, but when he was away it was different.

I went home once during the time I lived there, when my mother was dying, but I did not leave the children with Fedo – he would have refused in any case. I left them with the neighbour, Arlotte. I wanted to come back quickly, but when I got home, Michelle asked me to stay – my mother was dying of the drink. I felt so confused; I hoped the doctor would tell me what to do. I could see no way out except by ending it. I can't remember the details of that visit, except that my mother died two weeks after I got home and I had to sort things out. I wrote to Arlotte, explaining, but she didn't reply. I returned to the caravan site, a month after I'd left, hitching all the way, wanting and not wanting to return, hoping and dreading that the children would be there.

No one met me at the station.

Arlotte had tired of caring for them after a week and had marched them briskly back to Fedo, telling him to look after them himself. She demanded payment from him for having them longer than we had agreed.

I knew what he'd done to them when I got back to the caravan. That's when it happened. Their eyes told me, but I ignored it then. My children.

Losing It

Fifty-Six

The police were called to the Campsite au Pruniers in the spring of 1979. It was an anonymous tip-off that led them to appear that bright morning, with much noise and self-importance.

The caravan was silent, but the door was not locked. Hubert, rushing alongside, anxious to help these officers, had to be prevented from getting in their way. They entered cautiously, finding what they hoped not to find in the living quarters, nothing in the other compartments.

One leg, the bare white ankle sticking out of dark tracksuit bottoms, poked out from the corner seating. Her head was thrown back, and there was something coming from her mouth. Her arms fell heavy and dull at her sides. She was just alive. Next to her were the empty bottles, the dusty fragments of broken tablets.

They radioed for an ambulance immediately. Jane was already in a coma.

When the bodies were washed up further along the riverbank that evening, they began their work in earnest. The little corpses were checked over for signs of foul play, then sent for further examination. The policemen were upset by what they found and questioned Hubert fiercely. Where was the children's father? Was the woman they found the children's mother? She was very young, surely? Who would know about the family? Arlotte stepped forward, reluctantly, afraid of Fedo and repercussions.

The initial report from the pathologist was that both children were either dead or unconscious when they were put into the river, probably smothered. There was unexplained bruising on both of them.

Fedo was not to be found. Checking, they found that he was wanted on a series of minor charges. They half-heartedly pursued him for a while, but let it drop.

Fifty-Seven

Elsie gets close to the young gypsy girl by taking some money from her purse and putting it on a concrete slab. A pair of bright dark eyes watch her with interest. Another child flits past behind her. The girl gestures to the other child with her hand – don't come too close, don't go away – but she darts forward to pick up the money. Elsie sits down and waits for the child to come closer. At a guess, these are Romanian children, slight and dark. They will tell her about Jane if she has been here. Elsie reaches into her bag and takes out a photo of Jane. She hopes they will speak enough French to tell her what she wants to know.

'I want to know something, and if you can tell me I may give you some more money.' She shows them the money in her hand. 'Has anyone come here in the last few days? A person looking round the site?'

The girl creeps forward and leans on a post. She nods. Her dirty glossy hair is half-hidden beneath a scarf.

Elsie puts a coin on the slab. 'Who was this person? Young or old? Male or female? What can you tell me?'

'Not young, not old.' A coin is placed. 'Female, a woman.' Another coin.

'Is this the woman?' Elsie holds out the photo. The child creeps forward to have a look.

'Police?'

'No, not police. This woman is ill. She needs to go to the hospital.' Ah, they understand.

'She was here yesterday. At night. She was walking. She did not look sick.' This is the small boy speaking, elbowing his sister aside. He looks suspiciously at Elsie.

She takes a chance. 'She is loco, understand?' Elsie points at her head. 'Sick in the head.'

They nod, understanding. Elsie throws another coin out. 'Where did she go?'

They tell her, scooping the money up and fighting over it as Elsie scrambles to her feet.

Fifty-Eight

I am lying down now, on the river's edge, downstream from my old home, where the river bends and the sandy shoreline begins. They told me that this is where they found the children. I must have lost myself for a time last night. I don't remember it.

Very well, I shall join them. I am not mad – I am light-headed, yet clear-headed. Very lucid indeed, thank you, Doctor. There is a startling clarity about the world, a sharpness I perceive, as if all my senses are heightened. Which they are. They are.

How can I die? How can I do it? I want to join them, want to atone for their poor little lives, for my poor little life. It's a sad affair. Shall I wade out into the river and be submerged? Shall I float downstream like a dark tree, fallen into the river, in my funeral dress that Claudia lent me, now soiled and torn, my matching jacket ditto? I'm sorry, Claudia.

I can't wait any longer. The damp grit seeps through my clothes and I am chilled once more. Nowhere to go now; this is the end of the road. I roll the few inches to the water, wetting first my side, then my back, my other side, and finally I face the water, already nearly half-submerged. How cold it is. How cold.

Fifty-Nine

Running, the children alongside her, Elsie scans the riverbank where they last saw the woman in the dark dress and jacket, wandering without purpose along the wooded shore. Finally, around the bend in the river, they come to the place where the sandy beach begins. It is swampy along the path and they have to slow down. The children see her first.

'Look, the woman, the loco woman!' they shout.

Half in and half out of the water, unconscious, in a place where cold and hunger have taken her, Jane rolls her head in time to the river's beat. Her hair flows around her pale face in a weedy halo, dark as death. Elsie reaches her and lifts her head. Together with the children she pulls the body onto the bank, and begins to attempt resuscitation. Can she trust the children? She has to.

'Look in my bag,' she tells the girl, who is staring wide-mouthed at Jane's streaming body. 'Find the telephone.'

The girl dips expertly into the bag and hands over the mobile phone. Elsie remembers to offer praise, and the promise of more money, and pauses in her efforts just long enough to phone the hospital. The girl shouts directions to the ambulance over the phone, riding over Elsie's hesitant French with her husky young voice. Jane's pulse is there, faint and weak, like a half-dead butterfly. Elsie wraps her coat around her, sits her up and tries to warm her body.

'Can you find her something hot to drink? Is there anywhere here where we could find a hot drink?'

The girl shakes her head doubtfully. It is a long way into town. Her mother is away selling roses to the tourists.

Elsie has an idea. 'Are there fishermen here? Can you find a fisherman and ask him to help? A fisherman might have a drink in a flask.'

She searches her inadequate vocabulary for the right word and tries an assortment of phrases. Finally the girl understands. She speeds off through the trees. Elsie can hear, after several minutes, an argument going on upstream. The girl wants to take the fisherman's flask; he thinks she is trying to steal it. He follows her through the trees like a large lumbering bear, stopping short when he sees Elsie, supporting Jane's icy body. The warm chocolate drink is trickled into Jane's slack mouth and her head held up so that she can swallow. In the distance they hear the ambulance drawing nearer up the track.

Elsie thanks the children for their help and muses on the strangeness of life as she accompanies Jane to the hospital. Jane, who took the lives of her own two children, has been partly saved by two others. Dirty little scraps of kids who live by their wits and have little of their own, but who were concerned about the lady in the water, the loco lady who didn't want to live.

SIXTY

Elsie stays on until Jane has recovered enough to be flown home, handcuffed at the insistence of the Belgian authorities. They are met at the airport by an ambulance and driven back to the hospital.

The side entrance is opened. Jane, still weak, is wheeled in a chair along the corridor, past reception, where they sign in. Jane keeps her eyes closed, trying to blot out the reality of her return, anxious to avoid the curious stares of hospital staff.

Locks and passes, security checks, bolts and bars, all bring them nearer to the ward they left. Now and again an alarm sounds briefly as a staff member is called for help, and running feet speed towards them. The lino smells of familiar polish, and Jane sniffs the air, eyes closed, registers the smell of mashed potato, lino, Jeyes fluid, fear.

Back. Back to the place she left two weeks ago to go to her sister's funeral.

Now it's time to cry for Michelle.

The staff act with studied indifference to Jane's return. They greet her cautiously. John ignores her.

Jane comes into contact with the other patients at breakfast the following morning. Thomas keeps repeating "Jane's back! Jane's back!" until Ken quietens him. His twisted face is animated for once at the sight of her, but Jane is indifferent and speaks to no one. She eats little and sits, staring into space, for the remainder of the morning.

Sixty-One

"Please, lock me away, and don't allow the day.
Here inside.
Where I hide.
In my loneliness."

Back.

Back, and nothing's changed. I can't I can't undo the past. I can't I can't make it unhappen. How can I can I live on now that I know? No dream, no dream at all.

I had the lino fragment. I saw the river. I found the place. Changed. But still there.

And they brought me back, back to this place, this nowhere place where the sun never shines, where green trees never grow, where rivers never run. It's grey. I am dead, dead in the water. Want to be, want to be. Too late for tears, but still they run, pouring down my face like warm rivers over my parched face.

I am put to bed and treated kindly. In the only family I know.

Sixty-Two

It is the next day when Bruce hears Jane is back. They tell him Elsie found her, by some great good fortune, back at the caravan site where she used to live, and that she is in the hospital. He is interested to hear she is back on the ward. Moreover, she has asked to see him.

Bruce feels, when he hears she has been found, as if he has been granted a reprieve. He allows the image of his own mother's death, which has haunted him despite his best attempts to push it from his mind, to retreat naturally into the background. Second chances are precious things, he thinks. He feels sad his mother didn't have one. But he couldn't blame himself forever. How old was at the time? Nineteen?

Something slowly lifts from his mind and he feels alive in a way he hasn't for some time. He sends his empty coffee mug sliding across the table in the canteen. It stops just short of the edge. Energy; that was what he'd needed. And he has it now. He goes to find out what Jane's request is about.

Ken is sitting in the central office, gazing with glazed-over eyes at the monitor. Henry is writing a letter, with John watching him, hardly concentrating. Henry looks at the soft felt-tip he is writing with and seems to be chuckling to himself. Without warning he lifts the pen and lunges forward, aiming for John's eye. John, alert to Henry's impulses, manages to grab his wrist just in time, deflecting the black, inky point to his left shoulder, where it makes a black, violent mark. Ken is there in a flash, pressing the bell that will bring other staff to assist if needed.

Bruce runs alongside Ken. The frozen tableau which awaits them appears very strange. Henry, excited at having an audience, is bent over the table, his wrist still grasping the pen that continues to ink John's coat. His eyes tell the onlookers that he could have grabbed John around the neck if he'd chosen to do so.

John's face is white. He is using all his strength to keep Henry from pushing him off his seat. His right hand is still firmly on Henry's wrist, but he is pushing at an angle, and his left hand is useless to assist him. When he sees Ken and Bruce, the relief on John's face is plain to see.

Henry smiles his enigmatic smile. His podgy, unreadable face becomes more unpleasant when he smiles, Ken thinks, as he removes Henry's arm from its position and places it back at his side, prising the pen out from between his clammy fingers. Henry reluctantly abandons his weapon, and as Ken takes him back to his room, Henry turns and smiled at the staff, his gold filling shining.

'I wouldn't have hurt him,' he says. There is menace in his voice as the unspoken words fill the space between them – "but I could have done".

Sixty-Three

Bruce realises he is sweating as he finally sits down with Ken and Robbie to enquire about Jane. Where is she? She is usually about, doing something, with Claudia or Elsie or Marie watching her. He wonders if she is in the meditation room.

The incident with Henry reminds him of the incident with Jane when he disturbed her. These patients could flare up so quickly. He realises that they are here because they are unable to control their impulsive and dangerous actions, but it still comes as a surprise when they do this in such an unexpected way. His respect for the staff grows as he sees them trying not to respond with aggression, even when they are threatened. The two staff members look at him expectantly, so Bruce asks the obvious question.

'How's Jane?'

'I think she's become more withdrawn since she's been back,' Robbie replies. 'She seems to have lost the energy to do anything. If you taste freedom again after so long, then it gets snatched away from you, and you end up back where you started, it must be extremely hard to adjust. You know how Elsie found her?'

Robbie seems quite keen to tell the story again.

'Not really. I knew she'd gone back to the place in Belgium where she killed the children.' He almost didn't want to hear any more, but knew he'd have to listen.

'Elsie found her on the river bank. It seems that she tried to throw herself into the river but had become so weak that she collapsed and Elsie found her lying half in and half out of the water. She nearly died from hypothermia; another half hour or so and she'd have been dead, which is, of course, what she's always wanted. Elsie managed to get her to hospital in the town there and stayed on until she was well enough to be flown home. So now she's in her room, in bed, with Elsie watching over her, and she seems to have no desire to get up or do anything. She's hardly eating. I don't know where this leaves your work with her, Doc?'

He pauses, to see what reaction there is from Bruce. His request is simple. 'Can I see her?' he asks.

Robbie looks at Ken. 'Can we ask you to be very careful about what you say to her? Just keep it light and friendly, okay?'

'Thanks.'

He goes down the corridor to find her.

The small room has simple fittings and a foolproof window, door and furniture. Jane's bed is bolted to the wall. Her few possessions are in a bedside cabinet, on the top of which is a small vase with cherry blossom in it, picked on the way in by Elsie, from the ornamental shrubs in the grounds. Strictly speaking, they are not allowed, but Elsie decides that Jane is too weak to do anything further to harm herself and Ken turns a blind eye. The camera in the corner watches the scene unceasingly.

There are one or two small signs that this room is someone's home: postcards from Elsie stuck to the wall, a birthday card from the staff, two books of poetry, a notebook. These are placed on a ledge fixed to the wall of the room. Everything is designed with safety in mind. Bruce wonders what it would be like to spend your life in such a barren space.

Elsie is reading a magazine, her back turned to the doorway. She looks round when Bruce approaches.

Jane lies on her back, her eyes open but unfocussed, her candy striped nightgown in stark contrast with the sallowness of her skin. Her straight dark hair lies in damp crescents on the pillow at either side of her face.

Elsie rises and faces Bruce.

'You want a chat with Jane?' She turns to the bed. 'Jane, you've got a visitor. Don't tire her out, Doctor; she's not back to her old self yet. Are you, Jane?' There is no response from the figure in the bed. 'I'll pop out for a moment then.'

'Thanks. I'll just spend a few minutes with her.'

'I'll be along the corridor in the laundry room.' He nods to show he understands.

He tiptoes to the bed, careful not to alarm Jane. He did learn something from his previous experience.

'Hello, Jane.' No response. Does he dare touch her hand? The eyes become more focussed and she turns her head towards him.

'How are you feeling?' Safe, meaningless words which he immediately regrets. 'I just thought I'd pop in to say hello.' More meaningless words; still no response.

He thinks hard and tries again, hesitantly. 'Jane, when you disappeared, you went back to Belgium.' Checking the facts, a slight query in the voice. 'That's where you used to live, isn't it? It must have been . . . strange . . . going back, especially after having been in here for so long . . .'

His voice tails off. He is unsure what he wants to say. Jane's eyes are open, looking at him. He notices she has green eyes. She must have been pretty once. Green eyes, dark hair. He stays silent for a moment. Jane seems to be trying to make her mouth shape the words she wants to say.

'The children . . .'

'The children?' He is gentle. 'Whose children? Yours?'

Jane nods. 'The children were there. Playing in the trees by the beer shack.'

Now he is thoroughly confused. What is she talking about? Her children, her murdered children, or some other children? He decides to leave it there and check it out with Elsie.

'Would you like to come and tell me about the children? When you're feeling better?' The pale face on the pillow stays silent. 'Well, we'll see. I'll pop in tomorrow to check how you're getting on.'

He rises from the stool and stands over Jane. Is it his imagination, or does she flinch, ever so slightly?

'I'll see you tomorrow, then,' he says.

Sixty-Four

The children play under the trees by the beer shack. They hide and run out; a little boy and a little girl, small faces flashing in and out of the sunlight.

Christophe and Juliette played like that sometimes, when Fedo was away, peeping out from the side of the van, tripping on the hosepipes, getting snagged on the washing line. Christophe's little legs still unsteady, Juliette's nimble and quick. Ah, my children, my babies. I couldn't let you carry on the life I had.

In that dark van, when the power was cut off, we trembled as Fedo cursed in French and Flemish, and the children cried, tired and hungry, in their bed space.

After I came back from my mother's funeral it was always like that. Fedo was angry that he'd had to care for the children; the children were cowed and clung to my clothes when he came near. Because I hadn't been earning money he was eager to get me out on the street again. But I couldn't; I just couldn't any more. I stood out there with the rest of them, and Hubert took messages, but one look at my glum pallid face put the punters off. They thought I was ill and were worried they might catch it. Fedo used to come out and watch me, leaving the children alone in the van. His dark eyes took in the situation in one glance. I was slouching, unsmiling, not looking inviting at all.

'Bitch!' he shouted after the fourth punter had passed me by, 'Show some respect. Get your arse out there. You're doing business, not catching a bus.'

I was no longer scared of the beatings. I was dead, dead behind my eyes; nothing could touch me. Until I came back early that evening and saw what was going on. And the look in the children's eyes. They were like dolls to me then, dead, with little faces painted on. I couldn't stop them clinging to me, but they no longer existed as people.

'Get off me!' I screamed at them, unhooking their

little fingers. Fedo went out, slamming the door behind him and I heard the bike accelerate away up the track.

I see the woman I was then, like in an old movie, putting the children back in their bed, patting them like puppies, face set and grey, eyes unsmiling. In this movie the children sleep. Finally the woman walks in a trance and picks up a cushion, slowly, slowly. No more, never more. Nothing now, nothing anymore. She places the cushion over the little faces as they sleep. Carries them carefully in the darkness to the river, one at a time, like sacks of washing, and dumps them in.

The girl's hair hung down, tickling my back. She was warm, but not moving. I knew what I was doing, what I had to do, but I wasn't really there. Can you understand that? I was me and not me. Dead behind the eyes.

I thought the tablets in the bag would do. Stuffed them in, handfuls of them. Swallowed the water and felt them slide down, lumpy in my dry throat. Soon be over. Yes, yes, I wished for the end, waited for it, longed for it. All safe now. All at peace. The dolls put away, the lights off, the door shut.

I'm crying. Am I crying? I think these are my eyes. I'm not sure, not sure of anything anymore. That piece of lino tells me it was real. The lino was the last thing I saw before they found me there, half dead in that caravan, and is what I went back to find. A memory. A connection. A talisman. They took it off me, but Elsie is looking after it for me. She knows.

The children are not dead though. No, they're not dead. They're flitting between the trees on the caravan site. I saw them, playing, chasing one another, laughing. Not dead. There are ghosts among the rubble and the derelict shacks, the burned out cars and the standpipes, among the plum trees and the chestnut trees that hang over the beer shacks and around the entrance. My words stop stringing together; it's too much of an effort. Weary of life is what I am, tired of thinking and feeling and remembering. And the nothingness of each new day.

Sixty-Five

Bruce is also tired. He sits down on his bed and takes off first one sock, then the other, slowly and methodically, as if in a dream. He drops them on the floor beside the bed, noting as he does so that they form part of a small heap of discarded socks, which Fran would have called slovenly had she been around. Bruce tells himself he needs to shower, but yawns and gets under the duvet instead, pulling the soft pliable mound of feathers around him. There's something comforting about the smell; hollow fibre doesn't hold that body scent in the same way as feathers. It needs a clean, Bruce decides, inhaling the sour, warm smell. His eyes close almost immediately.

He dreams. A woman is running in his dream, with him in pursuit. He runs faster and faster, but cannot catch up with her. The woman's pale dress is at times almost within his grasp, but he can't quite grab hold of it, and each time he tries, the slow motion, deep water running starts again, where his feet are dragged down with leaden weights and he is unable to move forward. Frustrated and panicky, he wakes, heart pounding, and gets out of bed to take a piss.

Jane, his mother, Fran – why are they out of reach, why does he have to pursue them, why can he never catch up with them? Why is it important to him that he should find them, stop them in their headlong flight away from him?

Because, he thinks, with a flash of insight, he needs them. His mother he remembers as always retreating from the world. She gave him what she could, in a distant sort of way. Fran – forceful, overweight, practical Fran – had loved him, he knew, but he had been unable to respond to her love as she had wished.

One night, feeling incredibly alone as she lay beside him in their bed, she'd realised it was over. Bruce was exhausted, sleeping deeply, out of contact, and Fran told him later that she realised it was like this most of the time now, that his absorption in his work and himself had become total. There was no room for her. She rose, dressed quietly and with resignation, and left the flat. Would he miss her? Probably, but she had a life to lead – her own.

When he woke the next day he was bewildered by her absence. He looked for her, but she had left no note, nothing. He waited until the evening to phone, and by that time Fran was sitting nursing the third of several large whiskies at a girlfriend's house, and was incoherent. It was his turn to feel alone. He accepted it, it was familiar, what he had always expected. It stayed that way. Hurt, Fran busied herself with other things and eventually forgot about him.

Bruce needs Jane as a case study; more, he needs her to prove to himself that his profession is worthwhile, that he can help even the most difficult patients. Other things come into the equation too: research money, academic papers, his credibility in the department.

He yawns, stretches, and tries to sleep again, but fails. The women, separated now into three, run through his troubled mind, like threads going nowhere. His mind pursues each one, twisting and turning, following one, then another. He realises, as dawn lights the dusty terra cotta wallpaper, that he is near the edge. Dangerously near.

Sixty-Six

John and Robbie sit in the nurses' station and watch the residents as they go about their daily rituals. Activities are limited; the potential for damage and deviousness is too great to allow for many normal activities.

Henry is playing patience with a worn out pack of cards in the day room, chuckling to himself from time to time. Philip is in the corner, watching him and rocking backwards, forwards, again and again, unable to find peace within himself. Thomas is sitting, turning his jacket sleeve inside out, then straightening it again, patting down the folds on his arm. He examines his wrist minutely, then moves to his other arm and begins all over again – rolls the sleeve back, unrolls it, smooths it, rolls it again, and on and on it goes.

Robbie, who can bear the tedium no longer, suggests going into the lounge to watch TV with Thomas, leaving John to watch Philip and Henry.

Both men are on edge. Robbie is pale and looks tired. He wonders how they'll cope with the additional patients that are arriving tomorrow from Crowhurst. Six patients which none of them have ever met before – it will be quite a challenge. The fire that destroyed their own ward, started by a resident, has left them temporarily homeless, and they are being re-housed until their ward can be re-opened. Numbers on this ward have in fact gone down in recent years, and in this small unit there is only Jane, Thomas, Philip and Henry in a ward built to house a dozen. Other patients live in the next ward, equally dangerous and unstable, and staff move between the two, sharing the gallows humour that has become a feature of their lives.

John knows that this is a corner of the health trust which remains conveniently neglected by everyone. As long as the staff are not downright abusive and the inmates do not frighten the general public too much, it will carry on much as before. Jane absconding was a threat to that. Luckily the papers did not find out and she was returned within a week, but the matter had to be reported, members of staff had to be disciplined for their negligence and lack of judgement. As usual, the psychiatrists escaped.

John is still angry about the entire thing – the incident bred anger and distrust. He needs this job, and he was severely criticised for his behaviour, as well as subjected to several extensive inquisitions. His dislike of Jane has intensified as a result.

He knows Claudia is indifferent; she accepts it shouldn't have happened and is aware the rules state that two members of staff should be on hand for every patient. And though it wasn't her fault John decided to sleep in the car and listen to the Test match, she didn't protest at the time.

John knows Robbie thinks the new patients will be a real challenge, but he likes hands-on work with patients, likes to show them who's boss. The Challenging Behaviours Unit, with its autistic and troubled patients, allowed him to have a physical role, and this is much more restricted in the ward he's in now. He feels excited by the prospect of change that the arrival of new patients will bring.

Sixty-Seven

Morning again, and the staff are in panic mode, trying to finish last minute preparations for the new arrivals. Jane gets dressed, feeling slightly better, if still weak, and looks at herself in the mirror with a blank expression. She knows she's out of touch with the world today, distant, unreachable. She knows she will have to cope with the new patients. This will be difficult.

After breakfast – which Jane picks at – they begin to arrive, and are checked in, searched, and shown where they will be sleeping. First through the door is Arnold, small, with darting eyes and agitated gestures. Jane dislikes him at once; he's dangerous. With Arnold is Malcolm, his care assistant. Then comes Roy, tall and gangly, quiet looking, with an ominous scar on his temple.

Rahim and Dennis, pudgy, smiling, bring up the rear. Three more staff members come alongside, watching, observing, carefully steering with a word here, a gesture there, as the four arrivals find spaces for themselves. The door opens again. A tiny blonde woman comes through, hair in untidy wisps around her face, blue eyes looking up shyly through her lashes.

Alicia, four foot ten and six stone, stays away from the other arrivals, and her carer, Maureen, has to shoo her into the main area, where they will be told about the changes in their lives and shown round, one at a time. Alicia, thirty-one, yet looking younger than twelve, crouches down, trying for invisibility.

Dennis gets his cock out and begins to masturbate, and is told to put it away by Malcolm.

Robbie and Ken, making introductions and trying to contain the new arrivals, have to watch their own patients too, and so it is some time before the newcomers can be introduced to the residents and shown their accommodation. They are locked in and left to get their bearings while the staff meet and decide how to run the rest of the day.

'I thought there were six patients coming?' queries Ken, having cleared out a room previously used for storing linen for the sixth arrival.

Malcolm apologises. 'No. Sorry. There should have been six, but Martin had a massive fit this morning just before we left. So he's in the hospital with a nurse to guard him and he should be joining us in a few days when he's up and about again. You've got the case notes?'

'Yes, thanks. We'll need you to tell us a bit more, especially how they're likely to react to one another and which ones to watch. As far as ours go, Henry's the most devious, Philip's dangerous, Thomas is only a danger to himself – though he can hurl plates around when he's upset – and Jane, who's in the other female accommodation, is crazy from time to time – unpredictable. She did a runner from her sister's funeral recently which got us into all kinds of trouble, as you can imagine.'

'But you got her back – lucky for you. Supervised visits are a nightmare, especially if the press get hold of it when anything happens. Of ours – correct me if I'm wrong, Maureen – the one you have to watch out for most is Alicia. She's so tiny that people underestimate how manipulative and destructive she can be. She was the one who set fire to the bedroom and she's the reason we're here, really.'

'Do you know how she started the fire? It might help us to know so that we can take precautions. None of ours are arsonists as far as we know, so we could do with information.'

'We think she used a pair of spectacles belonging to a staff member. A pair went missing, and although we did the usual searches we didn't find them. Sunny day, a lens and some paper under the bed – it's possible. I can't think of any other way she could have done it. We're very careful about not bringing lighters or matches in, although some of the staff do smoke. We may know more when the investigation is finished. Made a real mess of the ward, even though the smoke alarm went off. The fact that the ward was being decorated and there were tins of paint stored next door didn't exactly help. I don't think anyone can be blamed for it. Maureen watches her like a hawk, but we've all got to have a break sometime.'

The two men acknowledge the difficulties of their job and commiserate about the high expectations there are of them. In many ways they are like parents, forever tied to deviant, demanding toddlers, who cannot even be trusted to go to the toilet on their own. It's hard work. No wonder they fail sometimes.

Sixty-Eight

There's someone in the room next to mine. It's an empty room, or was until they put the basics back in yesterday.

A woman in here, with me, that's going to take some getting used to. Daphne was the last, and I saw her off. Her and her dolls. I wonder what this one's like? Elsie, where are you? I'm afraid to stay in here on my own with her next door. Help me, someone.

'Jane, stop banging your head on the wall. You can come out in a moment when the new ones have been settled in. Read your book, it won't be long.'

I don't answer her. I scowl and sit still. It's quiet next door now.

Elsie won't want to spend time with me now that she's got another one to look after. I can hear another woman's voice, so perhaps there's a woman here to look after her. Can't see much. Robbie just went past, quickly, carrying something. The porter is pushing some luggage along on his trolley. They're going into the room next door to mine. If I put my ear to the wall I might hear something. They're unpacking her things. Boring. Let me out of here.

It'll be lunchtime soon, which will be interesting.

'Jane! I'm going to open your door. I'll walk you down to lunch and you can meet the new ones then.' The door is unlocked. It's Claudia, and I go with her down the corridor to the dining area, nervous and excited.

A small table has been added to the tables already out. Claudia tells me to sit there and then another big nurse appears with a child at her side. Then I see it's not a child.

She is introduced to me as Alicia. Alicia has flickering eyes that cannot stay still. Her hands suddenly dart out from nowhere, and she points at me, the hands like two small guns aimed at my face. I'm getting angry. Maureen tells her to put her hands down. She does so, but her strange, quick movements frighten me. So tiny! I wonder, does she speak?

'Hello. I'm Jane.'

'Alicia.' She lisps her name, says nothing more. Maureen tries to move it along a bit.

'Alicia, Jane has the room next to yours. I hope you'll be friends. Jane can tell you where everything is and help you find your way around.'

We eat, some sort of pie with peas and tinned potatoes, and nothing more is said. Then, without warning, Alicia slips down from her seat and comes round to where I am. She grabs my hand and smiles at me, winningly. I remember Juliette doing that, all those years ago. I don't want this memory; I don't want it at all. But Alicia is staring at me with bright, hard eyes. Maureen is right beside her, unsure how she'll be, and my hand feels uncomfortable in Alicia's birdlike grip. I'm frightened of Alicia, afraid of what she might do to me. Maureen tells her to let go. Alicia lifts my hand to her mouth, showing her pointy little teeth, and I flinch, expecting great pain as she bites me. But she doesn't, she kisses my hand instead, looking at me all the while. Then she lets go and darts off to the side with Maureen after her, and Claudia comes to find me. I'm exhausted, and ask to go into the meditation room. Claudia asks Howard, and we go down the corridor to the room. Alicia is watching from the wall over by the window, Maureen beside her.

SIXTY-NINE

I settle myself, sit in the posture, try to clear my mind of the noise and movement outside. Claudia is sitting outside, because of the other patients who might disturb me, though they shouldn't really be down this end of the ward. Breathe deeply, slowly, in, out. I close my eyes, try to see my mandala, my shape of rosy circles, try to focus, concentrate.

Faces, changing places, are what I see. The face of a little girl with Alicia's smile, the face of a little boy who is a gypsy. They are mixed up with my two babies, Juliette and Christophe, whose faces I forget, only to see them in the faces of others. I have no photographs in here, no pictures of them, except those my mind throws at me sometimes with no warning.

Alicia touched something in me; I sense the childlike knowingness, the primitive feral wildness of my children, runs through her blood. Like me, she has been treated as an object to satisfy the demands of others, to be filled up and emptied by them, grasped and relinquished, rejected and used. I saw this in my children. To me, they were like dolls much of the time. I went through the motions, feeding and dressing them, but only once did they seem real to me, hurting from the pain of what their father did to them. That was just before I . . .

This isn't working. Where is my calm, my soothing water music? It's spoiled. I have been punished enough for what I did, after all these years. Do I have to keep on facing it?

I know it's real now. I've connected with that part, but I no longer know where I am; I'm lost.

Before Michelle's funeral, it was as though there were a screen between me and the past. Then the screen was taken away. Dr Bruce started it. In Belgium I almost ended the story, wanted to, wish I had, but here I am, back again, and still labelled mad, still a prisoner all my life. What does any of it matter now?

'Claudia, I've finished in here.'

SEVENTY

I'm due to see Dr Bruce again today. It's going to be different. No dolls. He comes to find me, and Alicia immediately pokes her head round the corner. Nosy bitch. She won't speak, only her name.

Bruce turns to her. 'It's not your turn, Alicia. I'm seeing Jane today.'

Maureen hauls her away. We go into the room and Howard sits outside, watching the monitor.

'So, how are you, Jane?' Pleasantries.

'As you would expect, Doctor.' He raises an eyebrow at this. He hasn't seen me in this mode before.

'And how's that?'

'Oh, you know. Okay, I suppose.' He doesn't pursue it.

'It's been a while since we met, Jane, what with everything that's been going on. Last time we met in here we talked about a baby who was sick and you became upset. Remember?'

'It was all a long time ago, Doctor. It's history. No going back.'

'You went back, Jane. You went back to where it happened. What made you do that?'

Does he really want to know? I'm not playing his games any longer.

'I killed my children.' Cold, dispassionate Jane.

Bruce swallows. 'You killed your children.' He repeats the words, experimentally, hearing himself say them. 'You wanted to see where it happened?'

Not quite, I think, more to connect with something in myself. I can't say this; it's too difficult, too complicated.

He tries again. 'I've brought the dolls, in case you want to use them to tell me things . . .' His voice tails off. This is not how he expected me to be – something has changed.

It's me; I can't hide any more.

I try to explain. 'Doctor, can you imagine what it's like to be me? Do you have any idea what I've done, or why? Do you really want to know? I'm warning you, you'll need a strong stomach.' I wait, giving him time.

He looks a little defensive. Isn't it what he has always wanted, a patient who becomes sane enough to investigate the reasons for her madness, and who wants to approach the past rationally? Well isn't it?

He thinks long and hard before answering. 'You've given me a challenge, Jane. Well, let's try it. Let's spend some time each week going back over what has happened to you, leading up to you killing your children.'

He's being brave here, saying this again. It's the big unmentionable secret, on everyone's minds but never discussed. Bruce asks if he can tape record the sessions. I agree; what harm can it do me?

So we start.

Seventy-One

'I was born in a little town in Kent, not that far from here, in 1958, when my mother was eighteen. Michelle, my sister who died, was four years younger than me. I used to look after her a lot. My father was with us at that time. He was a bit older than my mother, actually quite a lot older, and he worked in a garage, doing up old cars and selling them. We lived in a small rented terraced house in Margate then. That's the house I remember, though my mother moved later on, after he had gone, into a council house, and I lived there with her for a while.

'Our mother used to drink too much, and our father and she used to have violent rows and arguments, mostly over money and her drinking. He expected to be looked after and treated like the king of the house, and she didn't do that often enough for his liking.

'Michelle was around three when the bad stuff began. It was mostly me that he came looking for, and I used to hide with Michelle in a cupboard, hoping he wouldn't find us. She was the one that told, eventually, and he was taken away and sent to prison, but not for long.

'Our mother wanted him back, but the social services wouldn't allow it. At least they got that bit right. Our mother never forgave Michelle for telling.'

'Can I check something with you?' Bruce asks. 'You refer to your parents as "our mother and our father" – can you tell me why you refer to them that way?'

'Because biologically, it's correct. I can't call them Mum or Dad, I can't even say "my father" easily – I don't want him connected with me at all really – but "our father" gives him a sort of distant connection without ownership, if you understand me.'

'I'm thinking of the religious significance of "Our Father" – it's the start of the Lord's Prayer, if you know it, and it goes on "Who art in Heaven". Is your father still alive, in fact?'

'No, he's dead; he died about six years after he left my mother. We only found out because a neighbour worked up at the hospital and told us he'd been admitted. Lung cancer I think it was. We didn't go to see him anyway. Frankly, I'm glad he's dead. Maybe saying "Our father" reminds me he is dead, though he's definitely not in heaven, if it exists. Which I doubt. While he was with us, we had to put up with his nonsense, but after he went to prison things got worse in a way, because our mother just drank more and she had men in who took advantage of her. They used her, and she was so out of it half the time that Michelle and I weren't safe either. Several times they would wander up looking for a chance to get it up with us. I used to scream and claw them if they went for Michelle. I was really crazy in those days, let me tell you, but I didn't let anyone touch her.'

Long, painful silence.

'Bruce, I'm going to stop there. Remembering Michelle is so painful. I did everything I could to look after her, you know? She was all I had left. And now she's gone.'

Silence. For a moment, Bruce doesn't know what to say.

'It's fine. Stop there and we'll go on another day when you're feeling stronger. What you've told me today helps me to understand some of what has happened to you. Thank you.'

'But it won't lead to anyone letting me out of here, will it? It still means I'm locked up here in this shit heap with fucking Alicia spying on me every second.'

'Jane, I can't work miracles. I'm sorry.'

'I know. Sorry.'

Seventy-Two

Sorry. Yes I'm sorry. No I'm not sorry. What for, anyway? I'm sorry for myself. I haven't allowed myself that, really, until now.

AND I WANT TO GET OUT OF HERE

and I can't

and the tears come.

and the anger comes after it.

In my mind they weren't dead, Juliette and Christophe, they were out there somewhere, like the gypsy children, playing under the plum trees at the river's edge. Going back made me realise what happened, and what should have happened and didn't, because they found me too soon. The act was unfinished. No, I just damaged my liver good and proper, stayed in a coma for a while. Then they took me back to England. I can't remember that time; I must have been completely out of it. I didn't know where I was or what had happened to me when I did come round, and it was Michelle sitting with me that got me going again. As I was unfit to plead, I was tried in my absence, and they never did find Fedo, though Arlotte had seen him ride away on his bike earlier that evening, and the children had been alive then, because she'd heard them crying. So he was off the hook, and I was banged up, for ever and ever amen.

The anger subsides a bit. I come out of my room and ask to go to the meditation room, and Elsie shows me down the corridor, checking me in with Howard.

Losing It

Seventy-Three

Here I am again, trying to relax, concentrate, unwind, be still. It's not easy. Dr Bruce probably needs this more than I do.

Breathe in, hold it; breathe out. It's simple really, being in charge of the central function of the body. Continuez. In. Hold it. Out.

Open sea ahead, waves frothing and rolling, as I dip and rise, dip and rise. As I rise I see land far off in the distance, like a promise. My freedom. It calls to me, and I float on the tide towards it. Let it be.

I let my mind go back. A walk in the park, under the cherry trees, their pink petals drifting over the walkways. Nan is holding my hand and pushing the pushchair with Michelle in it. Michelle is little, under a year old, and her cheeks are red from excitement and because she's teething. She's wearing a little corduroy suit with a zip up the front, but you know by her curls she's a girl. She loves coming out with us.

Nan points to the ducks on the lake and we stop to watch them. Nan takes my hand away when I pick my nose. I've got my boots on, but they're tight. Mum hasn't taken me to get new shoes for a long time. Nan will buy some for me, out of her savings. Nan takes us where she works sometimes, at the bus depot, so all the drivers can be nice to us. They ruffle up Michelle's hair and I hate it and want to go home. Nan cooks for the drivers, behind a big metal counter, cutting portions of pie from the deep aluminium trays out of the oven, pouring gravy from a metal jug, ladling peas and potatoes with big metal spoons. Everything made of metal and clean as a whistle. We are given treats by the drivers, Flying saucers, pink shrimps and sweet cigarettes. Nan doesn't like us having sherbet fountains or lollies because of the mess they make. She is also worried about Michelle choking on anything hard. The drivers do as they're told when nan is about.

Nan walks us through the park, pointing out things to see, lets us stop and look at things. Michelle walks a little way, holding my hand and nan's, staggering a bit because she's only just learning. She sits down on her bottom suddenly, as her legs go wobbly, and she cries. Nan puts her back in the pushchair and we start to walk home.

Nan used to come up to our house after work most days, in the afternoons, to take us out. Our mother would be in bed but she would get up when nan was coming and make our dinner. I used to get the breakfast for us most days. Nan and my mother didn't speak much. I don't know why things got that bad, but I don't think nan was happy about our mother marrying our father. She used to refer to our father as "he" and "him", never by his name or title. I think he hated her too; he used to walk out when she came round.

We were happy to be with our nan. She wasn't very loving towards us, but she saw that we came to no harm, took us out and made our tea; a distinct improvement on our mother. I suppose we did know she loved us. She gave our lives some shape and stability, when our father was always working or getting angry with our mother, who was either drunk or exhausted. That's what she always said when nan asked if she wanted to come out with us. "I'm exhausted, I think I'll lie down". As I said, they didn't talk much. Nan disapproved of our mother's drinking as well. "In front of the children too", she would say, as our mother tucked a bottle back in its hiding place where nan had discovered it, "You should be ashamed. Well, you've made your own bed, so now you'll have to lie on it".

I'm getting near the awful bit here, and I want to stay with the walk, the park, the trees, Michelle alive and babyfaced, me little and chattering to nan, learning poems she used to recite to us. "Don't care was made to care" was one of those she was fond of quoting, especially to my mother.

'Jane, time to come back now.' It's Ken, good old Ken, come to fetch me.

Seventy-Four

I can't use the shower because fucking Alicia's in there, with that Maureen guarding the door. Maureen stands there, her arms folded across her big tits, her large feet solidly placed either side of her in their sturdy shoes with the velcro fastenings. I can hear Alicia cackling. Maureen starts and darts forward, and suddenly there's a crash as she slips on the wet floor.

'Alicia, stop that at once,' Maureen shouts as she gets up. 'Oh no you don't, Madam. Give that to me.'

I look in, while other staff run over. Maureen is back on her feet. Alicia has the soap in her hand and she's stuffing it up inside herself. It's disgusting.

I shout. 'Ugh! Dirty bitch, Alicia!'

'Come away, Jane. It's none of your business. Come away. Now.'

Alicia looks at me slyly, her skinny body all soapy and wet, the bar of soap now in Maureen's hand. Alicia's nakedness is like a child's nakedness. She doesn't care who sees her. Alicia's look says "Don't say you don't get excited by me". And I can't, because I do. And I detest it.

I have to go to bed without a shower and I hate Alicia for it.

Elsie says, 'Never mind, it won't kill you for once not to have a shower.'

But I sulk and turn away. No one is interested in me now that Alicia's come.

In my room I hear Alicia chuckling crazily to herself. Maureen is stern with her. The night staff come on duty and we get shut into our rooms for the night, the doors locked.

I take a tablet to help me sleep – voluntarily. Alicia has to be made to take hers.

Losing It

Seventy-Five

Bruce is now uncertain how to be with Jane. She seems so different from the person she was. She's talking freely about her past, and to be honest it upsets him. He'd rather hear her talk in riddles, acting out that past in the game of charades their therapy had become. He isn't used to the bald reality of her previous life, so openly discussed now, without affect or self-pity.

Bruce feels swamped by the bleakness of her life, especially her accusation at the end. She wouldn't ever leave, he was sure of that. No one could say for certain she was cured, whatever that meant, nor could anyone ever be sure her violent extremes had been moderated to a point where she was safe to go about her business in the outside world. And again, if a prisoner has no hope of release, what's the point of trying to act like a sane and reasonable individual? It'll get you nowhere; there are few rewards here for good behaviour. Freedom certainly isn't one of them.

Musing, Bruce prepares for the day ahead. It's a mixture of things as always: a meeting with Dr Khan first thing, a ward round with the geriatric patients, lunch with Joe – if Joe's not tied up – dealing with emergencies and queries from staff as they arise, then up to the secure ward and a session with Jane, followed by drug reviews and his usual meeting with the Mental Health Emergency Team, to whom he may be attached at a later date if all goes well.

He's decided to think about support for himself. Something a member of staff said to him at a party still rankles, about people like him wanting to help everybody else and being unable to help themselves, or seek help from others. He knows it's true, but doesn't want to give in to the notion that he's been struggling for a long time to keep himself from going under.

The meeting with Dr Khan touches on Jane. Bruce realises that the pressure on him from staff has died away now they have other patients to worry about. In fact he almost felt welcome the other day when he went to see her. Dr Khan is happy to shelve it for the time being, he was only really concerned about staff hostility; now it has lessened he'll let it ride.

Joe does not show up for lunch. His group of girls and the arrival of two emergency cases makes him too late for his arranged meeting with Bruce, who sits eating something called "chicken curry" without interest, and tries to relax. Two ward staff come in but sit on a table together, and again he feels excluded and unhappy, though perversely he realises it would have been difficult to talk to them anyway, as he doesn't know them outside the ward. Eventually he gives up waiting for Joe and wanders up to the ward to see Jane. He regrets the curry; already he's sure he smells of garlic. Jane will probably notice.

He passes the security check and fetches his tape recorder from the locked store. Someone has put a box of toilet rolls on top of it. He tries not to think it has been done deliberately, as a way of showing him disrespect. Stop it, he thinks, you're becoming paranoid.

Howard goes to fetch Jane, who is writing something in her room. She glances up at Bruce as he stands behind Howard, waiting for her to come. Together all three walk down the corridor to the interview room. Bruce plugs in his tape recorder and tests the volume on the recording control. Jane sits opposite, waiting. He tries to gauge her mood and fails. She is giving nothing away.

Seventy-Six

'Hello, Jane.' Silence. 'Where do you want to start today?' Silence. 'You were telling me about where you lived in Margate and about your parents?' Jane nods.

Bruce keeps quiet. It's an effort. The tape recorder is running and there's not a word from her on it. He waits patiently until she speaks.

'I may have given you the wrong impression last time – that it was all terrible at home and everything. But there were some days I remember, when Michelle and I were very little, that weren't so bad. Mostly that's to do with our nan. She used to take us out in the afternoons, to get us away from our mother. She worked in a bus depot and she used to take us there. The drivers were always kind to us. She took us for walks in the park too, she used to let us feed the ducks and she was, you know – there. Our mother was a little frightened of her, because Nan used to have a go at her about her drinking.'

There's silence again and Bruce doesn't know what to say. Finally he chances a comment. 'You remember your nan as somebody special in your lives, somebody who you could count on to be there, even if your mother was drunk?' Jane nods.

The silence is so uncomfortable, Bruce feels he has to continue. 'How long did she carry on looking after you like that?'

'Until I was about four or five I think. I don't remember that time very clearly, just the walks in the park and the drivers giving us sweets.'

'What happened then? Why did Nan stop? Can you tell me?' Silence again. Bruce waits.

'One day, our nan came to fetch us a bit early. Michelle and me, we were in the bedroom. Our mother told us to stay there. I had to look after Michelle, I had to do everything for her, change her nappy, give her breakfast, play with her.'

'That must have been difficult when you were only little yourself?'

Jane nods.

'I learned quickly, my nan said. Nan came in and the house was a tip as usual, and Michelle's nappies were stinking the place out. My mother had a man in the bedroom with her, a neighbour, who used to buy her cheap spirits in exchange for sex. Well, Nan went up the wall when she found them, and there was a shouting match and it ended with Nan walking out and our mother refusing to let her see us. She died of cancer the year after, and we only saw her once after the row. She knew she was dying and she came to the door asking to see us, but our mother wouldn't let her in. I don't think she knew how ill Nan was, but I'll never forgive her for that, never.'

'You must have missed her a lot.'

Jane nods, dumbly. Did she cry when she knew her nan was dead? She doesn't remember. Tears of stone are blocking her eyes, giving her a headache.

Bruce feels her sorrow and realises there is a tear in his eye too. They sit in silence. He is momentarily lost for words.

'But somehow life carried on?'

'Yes, if you could call it life. Our mother made an effort for a while, to clean the place up and look after us a bit more, but she never stopped drinking, I don't think she could, it was asking too much of her. Our father felt our nan interfered, so he was quite glad she'd had the row with our mother, but he was rarely home anyway. He and our mother used to have violent rows too. Then he went all quiet and started being a bit nicer to us. I think he was having an affair with someone; we found some letters of his after my mother died which seemed to be from some woman. He stopped sleeping with our mother – well she was often so drunk – and he started with us instead. So now you know all about my happy little family, Dr Bruce. I don't suppose anything like that happened to you. Sorry if it's shocking.'

She is provocative, and Bruce feels under attack. It is

shocking, in a way, shocking that in the Sixties children should have had to bring themselves up by and large, working around a drunken mother and an abusive father. But he knows it happens even now. He feels more uneasy by her assumption, thrown out like a challenge, that he should have led a life free from all worry and hardship. But does his life with his mother in any way equal Jane's experience? He doesn't think so.

He responds to the challenge. 'It is shocking, in the sense that children should have parents to care for them, but you're making an assumption about me that isn't wholly true. I've had my own difficulties to deal with; not as serious as yours, but difficult none the less.'

He looks directly at her.

Jane spits out her words, with venom. 'I'll bet you never went to bed on a mattress soaked in piss. I bet you never went without a meal in your life, either. Go on, tell me you didn't go to public school, tell me you didn't have a nice upbringing. You'll never understand people like me, because you've always been shielded from us. It's true, isn't it?'

Bruce is caught up in this now; he should never have been stung by her remarks so that he needed to respond. In for a penny, in for a pound. Maybe it won't hurt to let her know that he's not perfect.

'I know what it's like to have a mother so depressed she shut herself in a bedroom for days on end. I know what it's like to be sent away from my family, and while I was away my mother killed herself. She'd tried before, many times, but when I was nineteen she managed it. So, no, it's not been as perfect as you would like to think.'

This is unexpected. Jane is taken aback. She remembers when Elsie commented that she and Jane were both orphans – it's the same kind of feeling she has now, sitting there looking at him. Isn't he just another doctor, paid to sort out nutcases like her? But no, it seems he's real, like her in some way, and she's stung him with her remarks. But she still doesn't trust him. She gets up to go.

'So you couldn't save your loony mother, so you thought you'd try to rescue some of us, is that it? Dr Bruce, I pity you. No wonder you need people like me to practise on.'

Howard, who has been outside, half-listening, has registered alarm and is looking at his watch. Time to go.

Bruce walks from the ward taking his tapes with him. He wants to think about the session. He has stepped over some boundary line with Jane. Is it good or bad? He simply doesn't know.

Seventy-Seven

Bruce is confused about where to go next with Jane. This is not textbook Milton Erickson; no one took control over Erickson in the way Jane is trying to control him. As he stops at the ward entrance to be let out, Howard catches up with him and pulls him to one side.

'Dr Townsend. Can you spare a moment?' Bruce nods, surprised. They turn to face away from the exit so they can't be overheard.

'I couldn't help overhearing some of the session just now. I just thought I'd tell you that we have a policy here of not letting the patients know too much about us. It's for our protection; we get some pretty dangerous characters in here and they can use any knowledge they have, twist it around and come back at you later with it. Jane can be very calculating at times, you know. You don't see the worst side of her.'

'I've seen her angry, seen her quite violent in fact – I know it's different for me, I don't have to be with her every day, but I have got some idea of what she's capable of.'

He's on the defensive, not taking up the point Howard is raising. He took a risk, he knows it, but Jane stung him and he wanted to respond. Surely it couldn't hurt for her to see him as a human being. But somehow he should have known it would be frowned upon by his seniors.

'We are all open to attack in different ways. People like Jane are past masters at exploiting any weaknesses they find. They've nothing better to do, and they get a buzz out of stirring us up. Do you see what I'm getting at? I'm only warning you for your own good.'

Now Howard is overstepping the mark; no one below a doctor tells a doctor what to do. But Howard knows he's right and he's doesn't back off. Bruce plays it safe, but is seething inside.

'I think you've said enough now, Howard. Sometimes we have to balance one risk with another. I can see that what you're saying makes sense in the light of your experience, but you're not in a therapeutic role with Jane, your role is something different, and I'm not around to be attacked by the other patients as you might be.' Howard's angry now. 'Dr Townsend, this is the only home these patients have. The day-to-day care and management of them is hard work, but in their own way those things are just as much a therapy as anything else on offer. They're safe, they're protected from harming themselves or one another, they have regular meals and clean beds and we do the best we can to give them opportunities for socialisation and all the rest of it. Without that they'd probably be dead, most of them, shot while holed up with a hostage somewhere, like Henry, or committing unspeakable acts in public, like Philip or Thomas, a danger to themselves and everyone else. We give them care, security and protection. What could be more therapeutic than that?'

He doesn't add that one hour a week talking with someone in a semi-private room is all Dr Townsend is offering as a contrast, but the unspoken thought hangs in the air between them. Bruce is silent for a moment.

'Unless these patients are safely contained, the work I do isn't possible at all, so clearly it is the priority, but you must allow some attempts to work with them, to see if they can be helped. Jane was chosen because she is more lucid then the others, and because she is capable of forming relationships with staff.'

Howard concedes this, but decides that he's said enough. No one knows what future promotion procedures might put Dr Townsend in charge of the ward – stranger things have happened – and he's said what he needs to say.

Bruce concludes with a parting shot, 'So, we do need to apply some different treatment models to them to see whether they could safely be released some day – supported of course – but released all the same. I've got to go, but we'll talk about it again.'

Howard walks away feeling that not only has Bruce made a fundamental error by giving Jane sensitive information about himself – which she has already attacked him with – he has now made a second error in refusing to accept Howard's warning as serious.

'I sometimes think the patients here are surprisingly sane when I meet some of the staff from other wards,' Howard says to Ken when he gets back.

'I know what you mean – who's been winding you up now?'

'That registrar, Townsend. Hasn't got the first idea about dealing with these people. Do you know what he told Jane?'

Ken looks blank. 'What?'

'He only told her his mother killed herself and that he'd had a rotten childhood – I mean, is that stupid or what? Of course Jane's going to use the information against him – in fact she already has. Accused him of not being able to save his loony mother, so he was trying to save her. Personally, I think she was spot on, but . . .'

'I can't imagine letting a patient know something like that. Philip would use it; he'd go to town on it. He'd buy a Mother's Day card if he could, and write some cruel message inside, then give it to Bruce. The poor sod's so naive he wouldn't realise until too late what was happening.'

'Better get moving or they'll be yelling for their tea.'

'I suppose so.'

They put aside the discussion and set about getting the afternoon drinks for the patients. None of the drinks will be boiling hot, or have teaspoons in, or teabags. These are the rules here, and now, with the added numbers, they have to be even more vigilant.

Rahim, who likes tea with a lot of sugar and no milk, throws his drink – which contains milk and no sugar – over Thomas. Staff jump in hastily to sort them out. Rahim is pacified, Thomas is moved to another table, where he breaks his biscuit into a million tiny crumbs, then licks his thumb and picks them up, speck by speck. For the umpteenth time this week, the staff muse on the fact that it would drive you crazy if you weren't already.

Alicia peeks coquettishly over her mug of tea at Ken,

who feels uneasy and tries to start a conversation with Rahim. Arnold, on another table, is agitated because he isn't used to these resident patients who know the ropes in this ward. He's the newcomer here and he feels it acutely. His restless eyes miss nothing. He and Alicia are old enemies, being very much alike in some way. The medication has not slowed them down; they remain twitchy and impulsive, but no doubt this can be medicated out of them eventually.

Arnold is small and wiry, the connecting neurones in his brain have been wrongly wired and fused together by genetics and drugs – both his own and those his doctors have given him. There's no telling what he might do, or when. He was never "normal", and will never be so.

Arnold drinks his tea, pulling faces, then starts to rock backwards and forwards. Malcolm, his key worker, tells him to get up, knowing that rocking is a prelude to something else, usually explosive, almost always dangerous. Arnold walks with Malcolm, protesting, to the television room. The other residents drift away from the tables and are taken to different areas by staff to play board games.

Jane is bored, as she usually is, and thinks about what's on offer. None of it seems appealing.

Seventy-Eight

I am thinking about what Dr Bruce told me. What does it mean? His mother killed herself. I can't get over that, it's weird. Not that she killed herself, but that Dr Bruce should have come out with it like that. Do I feel sorry for him? I don't know. It's something that unsettles me. He is in some way like me, has suffered too, only he seems to have come to terms with it better. It's an area that's difficult to think about. It changes things. He has stopped being just a doctor and I don't know if I can cope with that.

Nobody except my nan ever showed me love. I don't know what it is really. I watch films on TV and I can't identify with the characters who are supposed to be in love.

I think my mother loved me once, when I was very small, but then she started drinking and nan sort of took over after that, when Michelle was born.

I remember going up to my mother one day as she lay on the sofa in our front room. I tugged her arm, the way Juliette used to tug at mine, to make her pay attention. I think someone was at the door. She told me to go and see who was there. Michelle slipped past me and ran out towards the road as I opened the door. The postman, who was at the door, caught hold of her, and shouted at our mother to come and sign for a parcel, then pushed Michelle back into the house. I stood there barring the way until finally my mother staggered to the door and nudged me aside.

We wanted to see what was in the parcel and tried to help her open it, excited for her, hoping she would be pleased. Inside was a bundle of secondhand clothes for us from our cousin, and a birthday card to my mother with a brooch pinned to it. We didn't know it was her birthday, our father hadn't said, although he arrived home later carrying some flowers and a card for her. Michelle and I looked at the clothes and our mother sorted them into two piles, one for Michelle and one for me. Later she went down the road and sold them to buy vodka, but I managed to keep a dress, a pink dress with a lace edging. I never wore it, but I used to get it out and look at it sometimes. It was all I had.

Love. What is it? The nearest I've come to finding something like it has been here. Elsie cares, she looks after me, and is more of a mother than anyone I've known.

Fedo, so cruel and self-interested, was never affectionate, but he wanted me and he was attractive. He was strong and in control, and he was different from our father. He offered me an escape route from my mother's house and in exchange I became his property. People were things to him, to be used for his own purposes. At first I mistook his sexual demands for love, but I soon learned that, like me, he had never known love. This was the thing which bound us together and which I understood only too well. I built a wall around myself which no one could climb, not even my children.

When I think of Fedo, I feel a kind of numb hatred, like the weight of a stone in my heart. I'm here because of what he did, because of what the children and I went through and couldn't deal with. It seemed the best – the only – thing to do at the time, and because of it I am here, for the rest of my life, for ever and ever amen.

As for what my father offered, that wasn't love, though he pretended it was. It was attention of a kind, and God knows we needed that after our nan died.

I shall tell Dr Bruce about that when I see him again.

Seventy-Nine

I'm back in the meditation room again, with Claudia outside to stop anyone disturbing me. I breathe deeply, sit still in the position, wriggle my bottom to get more comfortable. This is a peaceful place, the only place where I feel calm and at ease. I have hidden the pin here, in a secret place, the pin that I picked up off the floor. It's like a promise, but I'm not quite ready to use it. Not yet.

Be still, be calm, breathe slowly, gently, deeply. Eyes closed, fingers curled, palms open and upward.

What is it like to die? To drift away, to feel the world shrink back into itself, like a distant planet. There is something I need to finish before I go, something with Dr Bruce. He will know my story before the end. Then the end will *be* the end and not an episode in the life of a crazy woman, condemned to see out her days here in this ward.

Concentrate, focus.

A man's face. Not Fedo. Small pudgy nose and red lips, coming closer. I can't look at the eyes, they stare at me too knowingly. I want to kick and scream, but I'm frozen. I let it happen and go somewhere else, to the secret room inside my head, where only I am in control.

A lilac tree grew outside our house, with white frothy cones of scented flowers which I would try to reach. It was a thing of peace in my life, a constant source of pleasure. I see it before me now, reminding me of home and what I lost. The last time I saw that tree was when I went back to England when my mother died. It was in bloom then, reminding me that what happened, happened. Lilac will always remind me of my home.

After my mother died, I picked some of the flowers to put on her coffin. Michelle thought I was stupid, but I told her what it meant to me and then I think she understood.

Death and love, this is what I think about these days. My mother's death was quick, though in a sense she had been killing herself for years. She died when her liver refused to work any more and she became yellow and full of water. She couldn't speak to me, but she grabbed my hand just before she became unconscious, and I wanted to pull it away. I was still so angry with her, for dying, for taking away any chance I might have had of a normal relationship with her, and for not having loved us enough to stop her drinking.

It was hard to cry, I was too angry.

Claudia knocks on the door. 'Time to come back now, Jane.'

I get up slowly, my thighs stiff where they were folded. I'm getting old, I can feel it. But not for much longer.

Eighty

Bruce and Joe are having lunch. Bruce is keen to know what Joe does when the girls he works with ask him personal details about his life.

'You know the anorexic girls you work with?' Joe nods, his mouth full. 'If they ever ask you about yourself – you know – private stuff, what do you tell them?'

Joe looks interested and raises an eyebrow as he eats, swallows and thinks of his reply. 'Hmm, interesting one. I suppose it depends what they want to know. I tell them I've got a girlfriend – I'd tell them that, even if I hadn't, because it stops them entertaining as many fantasies about me as when they assume I'm young and single. I've received the odd love letter, so I feel I need to be careful.'

'Really? What did you do about it?'

'Ignored it completely. Resist temptation, as my mother used to say. But to get back to your question, what was it they wanted to know?'

Bruce decides to be open with Joe. After all, he's known him a long time and there's not much Joe doesn't know about him.

'It's Jane, of course, who else? She challenged me, said how could I understand her when my own life had been so cosy: public school, good parents, enough money, that sort of thing. She was very provocative. I'm afraid I told her my mother had been ill for many years with depression and had killed herself when I was nineteen, and that I'd been sent away from home – I didn't say to boarding school, but she probably guessed – and so I hadn't exactly had an easy time either.'

'What did she say to that?'

'Oh, she came back at me all right. She accused me of wanting to save people like her because I hadn't managed to rescue my loony mother, to use her phrase.'

'Of course, there's not a word of truth in any of

that,' says Joe, smiling.

'Now you're being bloody provocative,' replies Bruce, smiling too. 'You know it's no accident either of us are in this profession. But it's not the whole story. What would you have said?'

'Guilty as charged, I expect. After all, there's no point denying you've been to public school and have had certain advantages which someone like her won't have had. Why lie about it?'

'I didn't. I suppose I felt it might help her see me as another human being and not just a doctor. Actually, though, the real reason I told her is because what she said stung. Unfortunately, one of the nurses overheard what I said and gave me a bollocking afterwards.'

'What for?'

'His point was that it isn't ward policy to let patients know too many personal details about staff members, because they can use it against them. I could see the sense in that when he explained. There are some pretty sadistic characters up there, and they play mind games, being unable to act things out in any other way.'

They sit in silence for a moment.

'Will there be repercussions?' enquires Joe after the lull.

'I'm not sure. Jane doesn't talk to the other patients much. I don't think she'll spread it about. Howard's different. I could just see him heading straight back to the ward to talk about it with the rest of the staff.'

'Well, I've got to get cracking. Anorexic girls wait for no man. See you later for a drink?'

'Why not? Usual place?'

They go their separate ways, taking the stairs two at a time and ducking the visitors armed with fruit and flowers.

Eighty-One

"I've got to get out of this place,
If it's the last thing I ever do."

When I absconded, I could have killed myself so easily on the way to Belgium. But I knew I had to get there. I had to know it was real, that it happened in that place, at that time. I was tormented by their faces, by what happened. I needed to know first, then end it.

They stopped me, they brought me back, but now it's worse.

I know I have to write this:

I killed my children. It was me. Not a woman in a dream, not knowing what she was doing, but me, this me, this living breathing me. I killed them. Me.

And I will not live with that knowledge. My own children, with no nan's hand to hold. I killed them because I couldn't watch them suffer as I had done. Better to end it than go on like this, endlessly counting the days. The daze. I'm sane now, as sane as I'll ever be. And I cannot live with myself.

Dr Bruce needs to know the reasons. He needs to know, someone needs to know, I have to tell it. I began, but then I got angry and accused him. He didn't stop me being angry. He told me stuff about himself. I need to see him, to sort it out.

I haven't been taking my medication, the one they put me on when I got back from Belgium. I've always been obedient in that respect, thinking the pills might help my moods, but when I was away I realised my head was clearer without them. I spit them out when they're not looking. I think Ken might suspect something; he almost caught me slipping a tablet down the sink when I washed my hands. He looked at me suspiciously but he hasn't done anything about it.

I still think about the children on the campsite, the gypsy children. Why were they there when my own children were gone? How could it happen like that?

I take a clean sheet of paper and try to draw my children. A sorrowful little face stares back at me. Is it mine, or Juliette's?

Did I love her? I think I did. I'm not sure about Christophe – being male he was harder for me to love. I watched him for signs of being like Fedo, or my father. Anyway, Juliette was the one he turned to every time, small though she was. She was the one who took him to play, who changed his nappy, comforted him when he cried. When he had nothing better to do, Fedo used to torment him until the tears came, and then call him a cry baby. Juliette would take him away and comfort him.

I was numb to it, and until my mother died I just tried to survive as best I could. Even when I kept money behind and tried to make plans to leave, I knew I'd never carry it through. He would come and find us, because I belonged to him, like a dog belongs to its master, and the kids were his because they were mine. I cannot allow him any ownership, can't say "our children", because he was never a father to them. My father pretended to the world he was a man who cared about his children, Fedo didn't even pretend. And he used them in just the same way as I was used by my father.

I can see their faces now I've drawn them. My children. I've gone past crying, it's too deep. Perhaps it's myself I want to cry for after all.

I don't know what to do with the drawing, so I leave it on the narrow shelf next to the bed. I want to do something with it, but I haven't decided what.

Elsie comes to check on me.

'Jane? I see you've been drawing – that's nice. You haven't done any drawing for ages. Can I look?' I nod, feebly.

'Two children.' Elsie looks at me carefully. She doesn't want to ask if they're my children. That's a subject we've never discussed. I nod again and she puts the drawing down.

Suddenly I want to tell her. 'They're my children, the ones that died.' I can't bring myself to say "the ones I killed", but it's there.

Elsie is careful. 'What were their names?'

'Juliette and Christophe, French names.'

'Ah yes, your husband was Belgian, I remember you saying. Nice names.'

'You know, when you found me, on that caravan site, that was where we lived, all of us. I wanted to follow them into the river. That's where you found me, in the shallow water at the river's edge, wasn't it?'

'Yes, you were cold from lack of food and being so wet. You'd spent a night out in the open before that I think. Do you remember seeing any children on the site? Gypsy children? They were the ones who told me where you were. They saved your life. But maybe you didn't want to be saved?' I shake my head. 'Well, having found you I couldn't just leave you there to drown – but I understand why you hoped you could end it there.'

I am surprised. 'Do you?'

'I don't have children of my own, Jane. As you know I only have Rascal, but if I had done what you did, and gone back to face the past – which I guess is what you were doing, maybe even without realising it – I'm sure I should have felt the same.'

'When they . . . when they found the children, they found me in the van. I was unconscious. I failed that time as well. The lino you're looking after for me; it came from our van. It was the last thing I saw before I passed out. I was bending over, holding my stomach and looking at the lino. It was the only thing I never got round to changing in the van, that lino.'

'I've still got it safe. I couldn't understand at the time why it seemed to precious to you, but I've got a better idea now.'

'I needed something to confirm that what happened was really real, if you understand that. It's the only way I have of knowing that I existed then, that what happened,

happened.'

    'I understand, Jane. I shall keep it safe.'

    Elsie's good, I can trust her. She leaves to get the bathroom ready for us to use. Alicia's been told about the soap.

Eighty-Two

Bruce comes back on the ward, feeling uncomfortable. He doesn't know what the staff have been saying about him in his absence. He goes in search of Jane.

Robbie stands by the door in case things get out of hand.

The session starts strangely.

'Hello again, Jane. How are you feeling?'

Jake looks at the floor as she speaks. 'I was angry with you last time, Doctor. I accused you of things. I'm sorry.'

'That's okay. Apology accepted.'

Jane wonders if that's it, that's all there is to be said. 'I thought you wouldn't want to see me again.'

'You were angry, but I'm still here. None of us choose our parents. I'm not going to apologise for my upbringing, but I can see how it probably looks to you. Shall we move on? You were telling me last time about your family, about your nan, and your parents. Where shall we start today?'

'Dr Bruce, I've been thinking about my father, and about what happened to me and Michelle. Could it have had an effect on our lives, on the way things turned out?'

'Why don't we discuss it and see? What was the most important thing that happened to you; what stands out for you?'

Jane is silent for a while, thinking.

'When I knew nan had died, that was terrible. We didn't go to her funeral. We couldn't speak about her because it made our mother angry. But I did miss her.'

Bruce nods sympathetically. 'And you couldn't grieve openly for her, because of your mother . . . Nan was your protection; she had tried to protect you and Michelle from the effects of what was going on at home. So losing her meant you also lost the one person who had tried to make things better for you.'

Jane nods, lost in miserable recollection. There's a

long pause before she carries on. 'Apart from that, it's the memories of our father that stand out. I remember the day when he came looking for us and found both of us hiding under our mother's bed. That was the day he started on Michelle, because I didn't want to play his little games. He called them games. But later, Michelle told our neighbour and she fetched the police.'

Jane is back in the past, remembering, experiencing the panic, the anger, the excitement of that time. They are silent, overwhelmed by the enormity of her experience and their collective unhappiness.

'Did you think things would change?'

'You always hope. But after he went to prison it was worse, because our mother went to pieces even more. Social services looked in now and again, but they couldn't do much. They took Michelle into care when she got older, but no one seemed to be bothered about me at all.

'When I was thirteen I started knocking about with lads at the amusement arcade – that's where I met Fedo, at the fairground – and I stopped going to school. Well, I went a few times, when we had English, because I liked the poetry we had to read.

'Our mother wasn't capable of looking after herself at all really. She was beaten by people she owed money to, or she would fall down the stairs and not be able to get up.'

'So you were frightened to leave her?' Bruce thinks he understands. Jane nods. 'How long was your father sent to prison for?'

'Three and a half years. He was out in two. He came looking for us, but social services wouldn't let him come back.'

'You were glad about that?'

'By then I hated him, never wanted to see him again. I used to feel sick with fear when he came past our house. I still can't think about him without feeling sick.'

'What would you say to him if he were here?'

'You utter bastard bastard bastard – how could you do that to children? We were your children and you did that to us. I hope you rot in hell forever. Bastard!'

Jane has nothing to focus her anger on, but her words fill all the empty air around. She smacks her fists down on her thighs, then on the chair,

Robbie, who has been half-listening, is alarmed by the swearing and Jane's loud voice. He looks in, but Bruce gestures that it's okay. He knows now that Jane needs to express all the anger she's felt for so long. If only he could do the same and free himself from the weight of his family's history, maybe he could be happier.

Boarding schools are not places which encourage emotional outpourings, and any signs of weeping or irrational anger were met at Bruce's school with a cold and embarrassed silence. He swiftly learned that it would get him nowhere, and there were compensations. He could put his anxiety about his mother to one side, since there was nothing he could do to help her, and his talent for sport meant he ended up with little free time in which to mope. Yet his mother still sat somewhere at the back of Bruce's mind, a diminutive figure wringing her hands and wearing a worried frown.

Jane is silent, purged of some of the anger. She rocks back and forth, her eyes shut, her lips clenched.

'Jane?' She opens her eyes and looks at Bruce. Her expression is unreadable. But she is receiving him.

'Do you want to finish for today?'

In a daze Jane rises from her chair and leaves the room, without replying to him.

Back in her room it starts again. Lying on her bed, Jane pummels the mattress and beats the pillow, as a shriek inside her builds from a whimper to a wild, keening rage. Forty years of stifled screams come from her mouth; the howl of a tiny lost animal, bereft of comfort. Her whole body shakes with the vibration, and the anguish of a lost childhood emerges into the daylight.

Alicia is there first, with Maureen hot on her heels, and she bends over at the head of the bed and strokes Jane's hair, as a child would do to its mother, uncertain and afraid.

Maureen, unsure how to respond, watches her

closely. Alicia, in her little baby girl voice, is trying to comfort Jane.

'There, there,' she intones. 'Make it all better.'

Maureen, suspicious, tells her to leave Jane alone. The shriek has subsided into dry sobs and moaning, with some thrashing about and pillow beating. Robbie, who came promptly after the shriek reached him, watches with interest. Jane is not ripping up her duvet, not banging her head on the wall, not damaging anything; he hasn't seen her able to cope with such rage before. Bruce, concerned, watches from the other end of the ward, unsure whether he can be of assistance or not. On balance, he thinks not, and he goes about his other work with her shriek still ringing in his ears.

Eighty-Three

Alicia dances away from Jane's room, with Maureen following. Other patients have moved across the ward, skirting round with their backs to the walls: sidling, shuffling, darting.

Arnold smiles to himself and watches from a distance, while Thomas goes to the edge of the door and peers round, frightened by the uproar.

Elsie, arriving on shift, goes to Jane and closes the door to shut out the inquisitive. She sits beside her, and like Alicia, feels a need to touch her to offer comfort. But she doesn't, feeling unsure whether this will provoke a fresh outburst.

'Jane? It's me, Elsie. Calm down now, you're all right. Jane?'

Jane pulls herself gradually into a position that enables her to look at Elsie. Her eyes are blurred by emotion, her face drained of colour.

'Jane, can you sit up? Come on, sit up a bit.'

She helps Jane rearrange her body and notes how thin she is now, and how dead her eyes look behind the dark fringe. 'Can you tell me about it?'

Jane pulls the words out of a deep well somewhere in her centre, one at a time. It's hard work, slow, difficult work.

'He. Made. Me. Do. It. Bastard.'

Elsie doesn't know what happened in Bruce's session, can't follow on from where they left off. It's a mystery to her.

'Is this something you were talking to Dr Townsend about?' Jane nods. 'Something to do with your husband?'

Jane shakes her head, slowly, deliberately. 'My father. I hate him.'

'You told me your father was dead, Jane. I suppose you can hate someone who's dead, but you can never make them understand the reason, once they're gone. Are you seeing Dr Townsend again? Maybe you can discuss it with him when you see him?'

'He already knows about it. He doesn't know everything, but he knows about our father.'

Elsie doesn't want to probe, so she suggests Jane has a wash and she'll bring a milky drink to calm her down. Jane nods, dejectedly, grateful to have Elsie there to care for her.

Eighty-Four

I didn't know how angry I could be, how frightened of my anger I really was. My parents – not just him, her too. Why did she never listen? Why did she hate us so much that she locked herself away from us all with her drinking? Why? She had her means of escape. What did we have? Nothing.

There's a secret no one knows about, not even Dr Bruce.

Michelle wasn't the only other child in our family. I had a brother, born a year after Michelle came along. He was ill when he was born because of our mother's drinking, and when he came home he lived for three months. Our father wanted him to die because he couldn't cope with having a child who was damaged in some way. They called him Tim, and his face was a funny shape; that's all I remember about him really, that and his tiny hands, opening, shutting, opening, shutting, like he was looking for something he couldn't find. When he died, my parents told the doctor that I had lifted him out of his cot and dropped him.

He was crying, and I went to him because my mother said I had to. I picked him up, like I did with Michelle. But I didn't drop him. He did that, when he wouldn't stop crying; he shook him and threw him down on his cot. He went quiet very quickly, and when our father had gone downstairs I went in to look. Tim was very pale and breathing in a funny way. I felt his little fingers. They were limp and cold. The next time I looked he wasn't moving.

Was it me that killed my brother? That's what my father said, to keep me quiet when he did his business with me. He could tell my mother or the police and I'd be sent away.

I wanted to be sent away some days, but the thought of leaving Michelle was unbearable. So I kept quiet, and after a while I began to believe it myself. I didn't know that the doctor had put it down as a cot death, nobody tells a little girl these things, so I believed that in some way I had been responsible. After I had the termination when I was thirteen, I almost felt that killing babies was what I was destined for. Would others have done any better?

I have tried not to remember Tim over the years. Part of me knows that I gave him my small girl's clumsy affection. Part of me also knows that I was jealous of him, that I resented having the little attention there was diverted to him, when Michelle and I needed it so much. Perhaps I wished him dead. Perhaps that's as bad as killing him. I don't know any more, it's too confusing. I think our mother was secretly relieved that he was no longer there to reproach her with his strange little face and odd strangulated little cry.

They never spoke about it, my parents. It was never discussed, but after that I think my father moved out of the bedroom and our real troubles began.

Eighty-Five

Another day, another morning to be endured. Always the same, always the same routine.

I can't eat breakfast, even though John insists I do, and Alicia is at my elbow, tormenting me.

She tips her face sideways and peers at me through her bird-like eyes.

'Go away, Alicia,' I tell her crossly.

But she carries on until Maureen intervenes, then she cackles with laughter and throws her toast at me. She gets under your skin after a while. It's not as though you can have a sensible conversation with her, she just gives you little bits of things and then disappears.

First thing this morning when we were washing in the bathroom, she kept asking, "Jane likes the soap?"

I said I thought it was disgusting, what she had done with it, but she kept asking the question until Maureen came back and told her to stop. I don't know what she wants from me.

She flirts with the male patients, especially Henry, who seems to respond by following her around. He looks at her like a toad looks at a fly it's going to eat, eyes following her every move, tongue ready to flick out and grasp its prey. But Alicia's too crafty for him; she dances on her toes just out of reach, like a wicked fairy.

I talk to Dennis for a while. He sounds normal enough, but suddenly something strange will creep into his conversation and you realise you've heard it before, several times. It's to do with the film Psycho. Dennis tells you that Perkins isn't really playing a role himself, something has taken over his body and he isn't acting any longer. When I say that acting isn't reality, Dennis gets very agitated. He doesn't know the difference. He wants to talk about The Shining, but I get so confused trying to explain to him how different characters in the film are real or not real that I get confused myself and end up tied in knots.

Dennis has a mind that disappears down a labyrinth and gets lost. Mine was like that too at one time.

Bored, I ask Maria if I can go to the quiet room. She walks down and unlocks the door. I wait until I'm not observed and then feel for the pin I hid in the seam of the cushion. My escape route. Yes! It's still there. I don't need it quite yet, I haven't finished telling my story to Dr Bruce, but as long as it's there, that's all that matters.

Relax. Sit in the posture. Legs crossed, easier now I'm thin. Breathe deeply and slowly.

Tension is draining away. I say some words as a chant, which is what they said I should do, only I couldn't hold the words in my head then. I'm making up my own.

Green river running, soft water flowing, moving the barges,
taking me home.
Green river running, soft water flowing, moving the barges,
taking me home.
Green river running, soft water flowing, moving the barges,
taking me home.

A peaceful river bank, the sun scattering patches of light on the grass as the trees move in the breeze. The pale khaki water ripples and smooths itself, licks at the edges, little sips, and in the centre the current rolls the barges, and the scraps of wood and straw which float along in the current. Nan is there, watching the water, relaxed and in control of things. I'm safe while she's there. I dip my toes in the water, let the wetness creep up my legs while small water bugs squirm under my toes. It's warm and the bargeman has taken his shirt off. He waves to us from the middle of the river. Nan waves back. Something is missing, someone who should be with us. But they can't be with us, they don't belong, they haven't come back to me yet. My children. My sister. Tim.

Can Nan, who's dead, summon the dead to join her? Will Juliette and Christophe, so long gone and never truly mourned, forgive me? Not look at me with sad reproachful eyes, but with bold faces like those of the gypsy children? Guilt prevents them returning to me. My guilt. Mine. I killed them, after all. Even Michelle; I left her to go off with Fedo and she could not forgive me. I tried to be a mother to her. And I failed.

The river bank is sombre now, the shadows are creeping from under the trees and night is approaching. Nan has faded into the background and I am alone here on the edge of this wood, on the edge of this place that used to be my home. Alone.

Eighty-Six

'Dr Townsend, I loved my nan, and when I close my eyes I can see her clearly. I can see my mother and my father too – though I don't often want to remember them – but I can't remember my children. All I can do is make drawings of what I think might be them. I want to remember them; they get mixed up in my mind with the gypsy children who were at the campsite when I went back. For a while I thought my children weren't dead after all and that those gypsy children were mine – it's crazy, but it was as though all the years in between didn't count. I realised today that Juliette would be in her twenties now if she were alive. But because I can't always see their deaths as real events, a part of me pretends they're not dead, that I never did what I know I did. Going back there helped me to realise what happened. Am I completely mad? I do want to remember them properly. I want to feel they might have forgiven me, but I know that's impossible.'

'There's a saying that to know all is to understand all. I think they'd forgive you, but can you forgive yourself?'

'No. Never. Though there was no doubt in my mind at the time that I was doing the only thing I could to save them.'

'Tell me about your husband, what part did he play in what happened? I gather he was abusive to you and the children?'

'He treated us like his property, and he never wanted the children. He made me go on the streets in Belgium almost as soon as we arrived. He was greedy for the money, and even though I was pregnant he made me go out. He tried to persuade me to get rid of Juliette, but I couldn't, I was too far gone. I was very attracted to him at the start. He seemed to really want me to be with him, but as soon as I was away from England he changed. He thought he'd got me and he was going to make use of me in any way he could.'

'Did he mistreat the children?'

'If you are asking if he beat them, then, no, he didn't, though he used to beat me often when I wouldn't do what he said. Once, he found some money I'd saved so we could leave, and he gave me a real pasting for hiding stuff from him. He was a bully all right. He treated the children like he would treat a dog. I couldn't take it any more when I realised that he was doing to them what my father had done to us. I think I went quite mad for a long time. When I killed them it seemed like I was performing a kindness, ending their suffering almost before it had begun. I tried to kill myself at the same time, and I truly and honestly wish I had succeeded.'

'I can understand that. So you have no clear picture of the children in your memory? The memories you do have are mixed up with the gypsy children, and you can't quite sort out which parts relate to Juliette and Christophe and which parts relate to the other children? And you felt that in ending their lives you were saving them from something. More suffering? A life like you'd had?'

'Something like that. I didn't kill them out of rage or jealousy or because I was angry with them, I killed them because I could see no other way out. There was nothing else to be done. I suppose now, when I think back, perhaps I could have got some help from somewhere, but with my mother just dead and no one around to assist me, at the time there was no choice. I could not let them live the life I lived – we lived. It was unendurable, unending. Do you understand?'

'I'm trying to. I think so.'

'So I lost them both by hoping to save them both – and I hoped to save myself by ending it. Does it make any sort of sense? At times they've come into my mind, like pictures, and suddenly I've understood what the loss of them has meant to me. What I've done. The outside world sees it differently, I know. I read the press cuttings after the trial – my aunt smuggled them in. I think she wanted me to admit what I'd done and show true remorse. But I couldn't.

'I was in prison for a while, you know, and they don't treat people like me with any kindness, let me tell you. Then, if I had shown remorse, they might have considered me for parole after a while, but because they said I was crazy – and I was – I got put in here, and unless something changes in the system, here I'll stay. Except I have no intention of spending the rest of my life here. I blew my one chance of freedom in Dinant. I'm not going to mess it up again.'

'You plan to kill yourself? Is that what you're saying?'

'Do you have a better alternative? Do you honestly think it's an option to spend the rest of my life with Henry and Thomas and that Alicia for company? I won't do it. I'm tired of it. I know what I want and you're not going to stop me. No one is.'

'You know I'll have to tell the ward staff? What you've said?'

'Go ahead. They know it's always been a risk. I've tried before, lots of times. But this time it will be final, no going back. No stopping. Over and out.'

'Jane, is there any point to our meetings now? Can anything be done? I mean, what is the purpose of our meetings now that you've said that?'

'I want someone to know. I want someone to hear my story. You don't know it all, not by a long way. I had a brother who died – you don't know about that, do you? They said I'd killed him, but I didn't. I was only little, I couldn't help it. He was ill and he cried a lot. Our mother couldn't cope with him. I tried to look after Michelle, but she died. Did I kill her? I know it's not possible, but why do I feel so guilty, like I should have done more to help her?'

'Jane, we'll talk about that next time we meet. All right? Claudia, can you take Jane back to the main ward please? Thanks. See you next week, Jane.'

Eighty-Seven

Bruce writes up some brief notes on the encounter and goes to find Elsie to inform her that Jane has a plan to end her life. This will come as no surprise to Elsie, but the staff need to be alerted. Suicides don't look good for the records, but sometimes they're inevitable, and sometimes staff can turn the other way, out of respect for a wish to die when no other choices are available.

When Bruce tells her of Jane's plan, Elsie knows she will try to stop her, but she also understands, and in a way she will be glad if she is too late to save her.

She thinks about the river at Dinant and Jane's attempt to join her children. It was for the sake of the reputation of the ward that Jane had to be rescued, but it was purely chance that Elsie arrived when she did. Having found Jane she couldn't then do nothing. But sometimes she wishes she hadn't found her, had stayed dawdling over coffee another half hour in her hotel, had arrived later on the scene.

But maybe the gypsy children would have found her then and raised the alarm, and it would all have been one. Weak and dazed as she was, she chose her time and place, and would have lapsed into a quiet death, with hypothermia and drowning as friendly allies, carrying her into the river, to join her children, finally at rest. But it was not to be.

Bruce does not know at what point Jane will end her life. He knows it's not finished yet.

He doesn't know how he'll handle it when it does happen. She's the only patient he sees on a regular basis, and he's been through a great deal of turmoil to work with her. The staff, upset by his approach initially and inclined to stop him if they could, still regard him with suspicion. He'll have to tell them too, not just Elsie, but all of them, that he is afraid for Jane. They may prevent him from seeing her. He hopes that will not happen but realises he cannot stop them if they decide this collectively.

Howard, Robbie and Ken are organising the patients' haircuts – always a dangerous activity. The male patients are waiting on separate seats outside the medical room, which has been opened up for the occasion. Thomas mouths the words "Cut! Cut! Scissor blades!" as he waits his turn. For their own safety, some of the inmates have to have their arms restrained while their hair is being cut. The flash of scissors and razors excites them.

Bruce knows the staff can't be interrupted, so he asks Robbie if he can talk to them at their next meeting, in two days' time. Robbie nods his head, his eyes never leaving the men sitting in front of him.

Bruce continues down the corridor, thinking. Out of nowhere a small agile figure darts from a side room and grabs his hand, lifting it to her mouth. Alicia smiles teasingly and pretends to bite him, her tiny pointed teeth decayed by poor diet and medication. She's like a small feral cat, he thinks, startled and suddenly afraid, and he quickly pulls his hand away. Maureen is shouting at Alicia, trying to get hold of her, and Bruce pushes her back and thanks the nurse before walking with all speed to the security door.

On the other side of the door, he pauses. He can still feel her wiry little fingers, as if she's still holding on to him. He shudders as he looks at the marks on his hand and arm. Does he really want to do this work, he asks himself again, and he goes outside for a cigarette to calm his nerves.

Later that evening, watching television and drinking Special Brew, alone in his flat as he mostly is these days, Bruce starts thinking about his future. A dark fog seems to obscure his thoughts, he feels oppressed by his past life, his lack of friends, and by his chosen area of work.

What is the point of it all? He is getting older and feels he hasn't really begun to live. Jane has packed more into her few years of freedom then he has in a lifetime. He doesn't envy her that, God knows, but was his life so much better? He too feels like a prisoner, a prisoner of his own melancholy personality, unable to enjoy or look forward to anything very much, going through the motions and putting a brave face on things. He feels very drunk, and realises this will be the third time this week he will drink himself to sleep. Even that thought doesn't keep him from opening another can.

'To hell with it all,' he thinks, falling onto the still unwashed duvet, 'I couldn't give a toss.'

And with that he falls into a deep sleep.

Losing It

Eighty-Eight

I know they'll keep watch on me now I've told Dr Bruce I've got a plan. That's the bit they're interested in. Not, do I want to kill myself, or am I serious? No, they just want to know if I have a plan. I do, but I'm not going to tell them what it is – that would be pretty stupid. I know Dr Khan's due to come up and visit soon. He'll put me on some medication again, something different. I haven't been taking the chlorpromazine or whatever they call it, not for a while now. By rights I should be building up to a psychotic episode, but I feel very calm. Dangerously calm.

The other night, when I went to pieces, I got something out of my system. Without that I feel calmer, more in control. More able to do what I need to do. But I'm going to make him listen to the very end. He needs to hear what happened, all of it.

I miss the old madness in a way. It had its moments. It was exciting, I felt everyone paid attention, everyone sat up and took notice. Thanks to the local paper I was a celebrity just after I was shut up here, and a part of me loved it.

Evil Jane, child murderer, monster mother – all these things they called me, and I fought back against them, kicked and screamed, went out of my head, pushed them all away, afraid they would stop paying me attention if I calmed down. They used to inject me then with something to keep me quiet and stop me thrashing around. I couldn't think, and I started to drool, but eventually I calmed down.

Once I had, the events of my life would creep through the barriers when I was asleep or quiet somewhere, and I would feel the utmost terror. I was powerless and petrified. It was not an easy time. It took a lot of energy and medication to keep all that stuff shut off so it wouldn't get through the barrier. I wanted to protect myself from the pain of it, from my responsibility for it, from what they had done to me over the years – and were still doing, disguised as doctors. Something happened with Dr Townsend, and now it's happened it can't unhappen. And I can't, I won't, live with the consequences of that.

Free as a bird, Dr Townsend, free as a bird.

I go to find the other patients, and see Thomas grinning to himself, his hair cropped to within half an inch, Philip sat next to him, rubbing his wrists where he's been restrained, hair flopping in thin strands over his forehead.

Ken is on duty. Who can I talk to? I go and look for Claudia or Elsie.

Eighty-Nine

The staff review meeting is difficult to arrange. It means that all the patients have to be in their rooms, and one person needs to be on watch. The residents know there will be less chance of being observed during this period, and they make full use of the time.

Henry has made a hole in his mattress, partly for masturbation, but also so he can hide any little trinkets he may come across. A small button, a dropped coin, a discarded pen; anything and everything is stashed away in this secret compartment.

He has plans for Alicia, plans for when she is away from the ever vigilant eyes of Maureen. He will teach her not to tease him like she does. He has many fantasies about what he'd like to do to her. He used to have fantasies about the female staff members, but was happy to relinquish them when Alicia came along. He has always been afraid of Jane, knowing she's killed before, uncertain of what she might do. And Jane has never flirted with him. But Alicia, well, she is different.

Jane guesses, correctly, that she will be a topic of conversation in the meeting. Bruce is going, she saw him earlier and he waved at her.

All the staff sit down, new and old. They begin by discussing how the temporary arrangements are working, and Malcolm tells them that their own ward should be ready for them to return to in five days' time. Any problems are discussed, and Howard and Ken express their thanks that the emergency seems to have been handled so well by everyone.

The new staff concur with this view.

It is on this self-congratulatory note that Robbie finally turns to Bruce, who has been sitting quietly without offering any comment, and asks him if he'd like to impart any information to the group regarding one of the patients, namely Jane Pryor. Suddenly awake again, Bruce sits forward. 'I feel I need to warn all the staff here that Jane is contemplating suicide again, and she claims to have a plan. Now, she hasn't told me what the plan is – she's hardly likely to, after all – but I felt I should tell you so that you can be alert to signs of anything going on.'

It sounds lame, and he knows it. There is a polite but strained silence. He feels he needs to add something. 'I'd welcome any of your observations about Jane, it would help me in my work with her, which' – and here he smiles wryly – 'you will be glad to know, is coming to an end.'

Ken speaks first. 'Doctor, I think we all had major reservations about the work early on, and for my part, those reservations haven't entirely gone away. Now you're telling us that she's suicidal once again. What exactly do you hope to achieve by continuing to work with her? Clearly it isn't doing her any good?'

Realising that what he's said sounds more antagonistic that he means it to, he softens his statement slightly. 'Perhaps you could tell us a bit more about what you're doing and what you feel she'll get out of it if you continue?'

Bruce doesn't really want to go into it all again. He knows how it will go – he will put forward his views and aims and they will immediately counter them with their own – admittedly, highly practical – views and opinions, about ward management and the necessity of containing and managing these complex and challenging patients. Underlying it all will be the unspoken statement "and you're not making it any easier". He thinks hard about what he might say to get them off his back.

'Jane's a complex character, but she is slightly different from the other patients. She knows why she came here, what she did, and the reasons for it. I'm really just a listener now, she's telling me her story in her own way – it's how she makes sense of her life – but she has made up her mind that rather than live here or somewhere similar for the rest of her days, she'd rather be dead. She wants to finish what she started. You know that when the children's bodies were discovered, she was also found close to death. That's what she went back to do when she absconded. She wants to finish it off, that's what I'm saying.'

'And you're sure she has a plan?' It is Elsie asking. Although she already knows about the plan, she still hopes it isn't true.

'She says so. I thought I ought to tell you all so you can be on your guard. That's all I came to say, really.'

'Thanks. Any questions, staff?' It is Ken, asserting control again.

They shake their heads and Ken asks Elsie to do a thorough room search and then a strip search of Jane. Elsie is not happy about this, but knows she'll have to comply. The meeting moves on to the next item.

NINETY

Sitting and drawing, sitting and scribbling, sitting and writing in my secret code, I am shut off from the clang and clatter of the cleaners, the dinner trolley, the staff marching around the patients as they make their odd, peculiar, individual sounds. It's as though there's a glass partition between me and the rest of the ward. Maybe it's because I haven't eaten that I feel so lightheaded and weird.

'Jane!' It's Elsie calling my name. 'I'm sorry, but I've been asked to search your room.'

I knew this was coming, knew it all along. They'll stop me if they can. I say nothing.

'Jane, can I ask you to sit outside your room for a while, while I do the search? I won't take long I promise.' I move slowly to the seat outside, taking my drawing book and pen.

'Can I look at those before you take them outside?'

I hand them over, reluctantly. Elsie inspects them closely and then hands them back. She is formal and businesslike today. She has to do what she has to do. It's understandable.

She moves the mattress, prods it, inspects the pillows, the few belongings I have, even takes the postcards off the wall to look behind. It's very thorough. But I dread what's coming next.

'Jane, I know this difficult, but you'll have to undress for me so I can do a strip search. Do you understand?'

I don't reply. Silence is not consent, but it is taken as consent. Why does it have to be Elsie? I don't want her to touch me in my secret places. It's too personal. But the thought of Claudia or Marie is even worse. I have to submit, as I have so many, many times before.

And I don't even whimper. Soon I will be gone from here. Nothing else matters.

Ninety-One

Bruce feels a sense of foreboding. He has arranged to see Jane much sooner than he would have done before. This appointment is only two days after the last one. But it's a last chance – for her and for him. He feels pressured to hear the rest of her story, to finish something with her. Where is this pressure coming from? The staff are in no hurry for him to see her again. They are annoyed that he creates more work for them instead of making things easier in their management of Jane.

He is agitated, unsure what ending the sessions with her will mean, but certain he has to go through with an ending in order to complete something.

Ken raises his eyebrows when he takes the message that Bruce is visiting the ward today, but he gives in gracefully. As far as he's concerned, Dr Townsend's involvement has singled Jane out as receiving special treatment. What's so special about her, he wants to know? After all, she's not a very sympathetic character, she hardly speaks to the male staff since Trevor left. Now, if the good doctor had taken on someone like Henry or Philip to treat, he would have won the full backing of the staff. But really he's making matters worse, not better, by his involvement.

Bruce and Ken eye each other up, warily, as they pass one another.

Ken can't resist a dig. 'Doctor, you will let us know if Jane reveals anything about what we discussed yesterday? Thanks.' He doesn't wait for an answer.

Bruce is seething, but keeps outwardly calm. As if he couldn't be trusted to act professionally! It comes to him that the staff here make him feel incompetent most of the time. They act as a closed, self-regulating unit, resenting the interference of outsiders, and are constantly watchful, guarded and vigilant, especially towards outsiders, whom they shut out and close ranks against. This mirrors the paranoia felt by some of the patients, he thinks despairingly. Where does it end, this endless reflection process? A system set up to treat and contain madness becomes emotionally sick itself, confined as it is to rigid regimes and a policy of containment where change is threatening. And the idea of treatment becomes a joke, unless it's by means of drugs which the staff can administer and be in total control over.

Yet these patients are dangerous. Containment and secure confinement, humanely applied, may be all that is possible, given the staffing levels and resources. But there must be more than this, surely?

Bruce remembers his mother again, crumpled on the floor of the bedroom, paralysed by her fears and unable to function, irrational and helpless. Could anyone have helped her? Even now, Bruce is unclear about her diagnosis, but a niggling doubt in his mind says that the doctors who treated her had never tried to understand why she was as she was. They treated the symptoms but not the cause.

Would he have done any better? Perhaps. Though he didn't know enough about his mother's past to attempt to explain her illness from this moment in time. Maybe he should ask his aunt if she knew what had caused his mother to be so ill. Somehow he knew he couldn't ask his father.

He has to wait a moment before he can go into the room. Staff are dealing with Dennis, who has pushed his tongue down his throat in a bizarre attempt to emulate somebody he read about.

Elsie comes by. 'Are you seeing Jane now?'

'Yes. Is that all right? I phoned Ken this morning to let him know.'

'It's fine. I know she wants to see you. She's in a strange mood. I had to search her and her room yesterday after what you told us, and although she didn't make a fuss, something's not right. She's cut herself off from us all somehow. I think you're right. I think she does have a plan and she's just biding her time. Good luck with her.'

'Thanks.'

Ninety-Two

'Hello, Jane. How are you feeling today?'

'How do you think I'm feeling?'

'Sorry. Stupid question to ask.'

'I think this will be the last time I will come and see you, Doctor.'

'Why is that?'

'Please don't play games, Dr Townsend. You know why. I will not be here this time next week. You understand?'

'Yes. You did tell me this last time. I suppose I just needed to check that I understood you correctly. So where do you want to start today?'

'There's one thing I haven't told you about, to do with my childhood. It's about my brother.'

'Your brother? I thought there was just you and Michelle?'

'My brother, Tim. He only lived for a few months. He was born damaged by my mother's drinking. When he died, my father told me it was my fault, that I had taken him from his cot and hurt him. But I remember my father shaking him and throwing him down on the bed when he wouldn't stop crying. I did take him out, like I did Michelle, because our mother didn't look after him. But I never hurt him. I know that now, but back then I thought it was me. He made me think I had caused Tim's death. It was the threat of him telling the police that gave him such a hold on me when he did the other things. I really thought I was responsible.'

'But you were just a little girl, Jane. You shouldn't have had to look after the two younger ones like that anyway. You were given an impossible task. And then you got the blame when it all went wrong.'

'But Tim died. Now Michelle's dead. I didn't do a very good job, did I?'

'Jane, Tim might have been ill right from when he was born, because of your mother's drinking. If your father shook him and threw him down, or dropped him, he could easily have died from the effects of that. It sounds as though you were the one who cared about him and tried to give him some love, so don't be too hard on yourself. Parents are responsible for looking after their children. They shouldn't expect young children to do the parenting; they need parents themselves. What did the doctors say he died of? Do you know?'

'When my mother was dying I asked my doctor to tell me what Tim had died from. It was simply recorded as a cot death. But I felt guilty, all my childhood. My father made it worse with his threats. When Michelle told the neighbours what he did to us, I was so scared he'd tell everyone I had killed Tim.'

'But he didn't, because it wasn't true.'

'I don't know what's true any more. I remember thinking that my mother wasn't looking after us properly – my nan had let me see that – so how could she manage at all with another baby, especially one who was ill? So I did resent him. But I'm sure I never hurt him – not on purpose anyway.

'There's something else I haven't told you. I lost a baby when I was thirteen. I had a termination, because my mother insisted. It was a man from round the back of us, he used to follow Michelle and me around. I used to let him do what he wanted, he'd give us sweets and money and things. She never gave us anything, so I suppose we felt we could get things we never had at home. He didn't threaten us like our father used to, he kept telling us what good girls we were, and how grateful he was to us, so we thought it was all right.

'When I got pregnant, all that changed. He got scared and didn't want to know any more. My mother was angry and didn't speak to me for days. I never told them who it was, and Michelle kept quiet that time. They thought it was a boy at school we were friendly with. It was only because I was so sick at school that the teacher guessed what was wrong and I had to tell them, otherwise I think I would have gone through with it, just because I didn't know what else to do.'

'So once again you felt responsible for the loss of a

baby – first Tim and then the baby you were pregnant with?'

'Yes. Baby killer, that's me.'

'Stop it, Jane.'

'Child murderer, baby killer. Oh see that woman over there? She killed four children, she did. She dropped one, had another taken out of her so that it couldn't live, and then killed her own two children by suffocating them and dumping them in a river. And she's still here. Oh, she's locked up, because she's a loony, but she's still alive. Why didn't she do the decent thing and go ahead and kill herself when she had the chance? Why didn't she?'

Robbie comes in. 'Jane, either you quieten down now, or the session ends. Do you understand?'

'Jane, have you told me everything you want to tell me?'

'Thank you for listening. I won't be coming any more. I want you to know that it's not your fault. I don't blame you. I'll go back to the ward now.'

'Goodbye, Jane.'

'Sayonara, Dr Bruce. Was that what the kamikaze pilots used to say?'

Losing It

Ninety-Three

Bruce feels very sad and troubled. Robbie gives him a sideways look as he motions to Jane to go ahead of him down the corridor. He caught just enough of the conversation to know that it's the last time he will escort Jane to see Dr Bruce Townsend. He notes that the doctor seems thoughtful and avoids his gaze.

Jane goes to join the other residents in the lounge area, where Ken is leading a discussion with them about managing anger. Jane slumps into a corner seat and closes her eyes, exhausted. Ken knows better than to try and draw her out.

Dennis, recovered from his earlier mishap, wants to speak. Ken makes a beckoning motion with his hand towards him.

'Psychos get angry. They kill people. Like in The Shining? Jack Nicholson didn't want to be a killer, but he was.'

Ken tries to be patient. 'We have to remember, everybody, that films are not real life. Jack Nicholson is an actor; he has never killed anybody. When people act, they can pretend to do violent things, but it isn't real, they are just pretending.'

'Like when Henry stuck a pen in John? He didn't really do it?' Philip seems puzzled.

'I don't know what made Henry do that, and I don't know if he would have stopped if John hadn't caught his arm. It's important to be able to tell the difference between real and pretend violence, and some of you aren't very good at that. Can anyone tell me what the difference is?'

'Films and telly and that, they're not real. But it is if you have a war.' Rahim is trying hard to make the distinction.

'Good, Rahim. If somebody here hurts another person or themselves, so that they are wounded in some way – bleeding or bruised or cut – that's real violence. Films where people are acting – pretending – are not real. So suppose someone here – Alicia, say – feels like hurting someone for real, what should she do?'

Alicia grins and bounces in her seat at being included.

'Find Maureen,' answers Dennis, hiding behind his fist.

'Alicia?' Alicia nods like a good little girl. 'Find Maureen,' she echoes. Maureen, who is at the side, smiles stoically to herself.

Ken continues. 'Everyone feels angry sometimes. That's normal. It's how we show our anger that matters. For example, Jane was very angry the other evening, but she went into her room and punched her pillow, not a person. She didn't break anything, and she didn't hurt herself or anyone else. Did you Jane? So well done for that. Thomas, you still have a problem sometimes when you get frustrated, don't you?'

Thomas nods, sheepishly.

Henry's smile is sinister. 'I get angry with Alicia,' he says, slowly and deliberately. 'She deserves it. She torments me. Alicia's evil.'

Ken has noticed Henry's interest in Alicia and is glad she'll be going back to the other unit very soon. Henry is cunning and devious and Ken knows these sessions are wasted on him, but he has to try.

'You are to stay away from Alicia,' Ken orders him, deciding not to pursue it.

'Jane, do you have anything to add?' But she doesn't.

Of the residents she knows, besides her, only Henry has killed someone – by poisoning them. He was twenty-one and it was his grandmother he killed, by infusing hemlock water dropwort, which he picked with great care from the bank of the stream beside his grandmother's house. It smelt of mice, but his grandmother didn't notice – she always complained about everything anyway. A cupful of herbal tea with some hemlock in it at bedtime, and by midnight she was in agony. Henry had eventually called out the doctor when it was clear he was going to be too late. At the autopsy the cause of death was evident – besides, Henry was hiding in a cupboard in the bedroom, completely crazed and laughing guiltily to himself.

Philip has never been able to stop himself acting on impulse. He hasn't succeeded in killing anyone so far, but it's not for want of trying. Thomas has attacked small children – attacks himself given half a chance. Jane doesn't know about any of the others.

The group meeting ends and the residents go for their afternoon tea and biscuits.

Ninety-Four

Alicia sidles over to me while I drink my tea and whispers in my ear. It's something obscene about Henry's dick. I don't want to hear about it. Alicia stirs me up and I would rather not be reminded of my sex. I was used by men so often that the idea of sex with a man now, especially one like Henry, is disgusting to me. When I was young I thought I could feel something, some excitement, at certain times, but going on the game I realised that men are all the same in that respect. There was a skill in making them come quickly, more quickly than they wanted to sometimes. I would feel I had beaten them then, they had given me something of themselves, surrendered to me. I wouldn't let them kiss me, ever.

Fedo and I used to kiss when I first met him. He stopped after the children were born, but I saved that bit anyway. The punters could have it all, but not that bit.

The men here on the ward – the staff – are not too bad, except for John. John is nasty. If I did business with him I'd charge him extra. I was fond of Trevor, he knew me well and he treated me with respect. Ken and Robbie and Howard are okay, I sort of trust them, but Elsie is closest. She didn't want to do that search the other day, but she had to. I made it easy for her. After all, I'll be gone soon.

I say to Alicia, 'You're a dirty minded bitch, Alicia. Henry's disgusting. You don't really fancy him do you?' Alicia nods emphatically. 'Well you want your head seeing to.'

For some reason this makes her laugh and skip about, bringing Maureen over to see what's going on. We both smile innocently at Maureen, who goes back to her work checking the linen store.

Alicia whispers in my ear again. 'After supper, ask to go in the quiet room.'

'Why?'

'Secret. Mustn't tell.'

Does she know something? Does she suspect

something? What is her cunning little plan? I am consumed with curiosity, but we can't talk, too many people are listening. Dennis has appeared around the corner, masturbating through his trousers. John comes out of the nurses' station and tells him to stop, or go into his room. Dennis looks at us. He knows we saw him and the outline of his cock against his trousers, where it makes a pointed tent. He grins at us, then wanders off.

Is this any stranger than my life outside? When I was young and free? At least things are controlled here. Who was there to say "stop doing that" to my father? No one. Not all the madmen are in the asylum after all.

I wonder what Alicia wants? I still feel as though there's a glass wall between me and the rest of the world. I am protecting myself perhaps, finally. When it's too late.

Ninety-Five

'Claudia, can I go to the quiet room for a bit?'

'Not just now, Jane. Wait until Marie comes on duty. Maureen's off now and there's only me to take you.'

'If you open the door, I'll sit in there so quietly you won't know I'm there. You can watch the others from the doorway.'

'I'll ask Howard, see what he says. But I'm not making any promises. Marie should be here soon anyway.'

She goes to find Howard, who looks up at me then gives his assent.

Claudia walks me round to the quiet room, unlocks the door and sees me in there. She sits outside, waiting and watching. The camera is not working today. I take the cushions, feel for the pin as I plump them up, remove it under the pretext of examining a broken nail, then sit up in the posture, supported by the beanbag. I am so thin now. My thighs are hollow and my ribs feels as though they stick out horribly. Now is the time. I have the means. I have the willpower.

I open the vein with the pin, quickly, a swift rip along the weak spot inside the elbow. The blood's flowing now, nicely, warmly. Claudia can't see, my back's to the door. It drips, then spurts a little. I rip again, deeper. No pain. I am already dead.

I breathe deeply, relax more totally than ever before. I am going home. I close my eyes, breathe deeply and slowly.

The gentle movement of water, bathing my wounded body, carries me with it. The river where I walked with my two children, where I knew some peace, the healing river, with its trees and fish and ducks and slow meandering currents. It's where I belong. Alongside my children, in the grave I chose for them, in the grave I chose for myself, but never reached. Until now. Freedom. Peace.

"Going down to the river
Going to make me a rocking chair
And if the Blues don't leave me
I'm going to rock away from here."

Ninety-Six

A small figure darts along the corridor. Claudia has dozed off for a moment, is struggling to fight the tiredness she feels. Quick as a flash, Alicia slips into the room. Her eyes see Jane, her head slumped forward but still upright on her bean bag. A dark wine-coloured pool of blood has collected around her right elbow. Her fingers trail in its stickiness. It is soaking through to the rug and the cushions. Alicia takes it all in, feasting on it greedily with her eyes.

Out comes the lighter, with a triumphant flourish, and Alicia holds the yellow flame under the bean bag, then the cushions. The polystyrene granules burn with a gratifying heat, but Alicia has already gone, leaving the lighter, speeding past Claudia, who wakes and shouts at her, before seeing the flames burst into flower in front of her. Claudia shouts for help, then remembers her bleeper. She tries to enter the room, but the smoke is thick and poisonous, and she stands in the doorway, coughing.

Alicia returns, followed by Howard, who carries a fire extinguisher and puts the fire out quite quickly. By now the smoke alarms are sounding, and there's pandemonium as residents panic and staff offer assistance. Howard, choking, goes in to get Jane. She's dead, as he knew she would be. Only when he lifts her does he see the dark bright blood pooled on the floor. She's as light as a feather, and illogically he wonders why they hadn't noticed how thin she was getting. But it's all one now. Bruce was right, she was determined, and she has done what she said she'd do.

The quiet room had been searched by Marie, just in case, but a pin – who notices a pin?

Alicia, her eyes darting, is in the way, and they ask Marie to take her back to her room. As an afterthought, Howard tells Marie to search her. Arson is not something you want to happen twice in one night.

The firemen, when they arrive, find the green gas

lighter, twisted and distorted from the heat, in the ashes of the beanbag.

The fireman shakes his head. 'Must be an old one,' he says, talking about the beanbag. 'Still, even flame retardants won't stand up to a gas lighter if it's deliberately set up to burn through the fabric. These granules are a nightmare – no telling what damage it does to your lungs. Better get you to the hospital when the ambulance arrives. Pity there's no A&E here, really.'

Howard and Claudia are feeling very unwell. And a patient is dead. The implications of this have not yet sunk in. Does this mean they will close the ward? No, probably not, the damage isn't great, mostly just smoke damage, and it didn't reach far. Claudia remembers that Alicia ran past her as it happened. She blames Alicia without even thinking about it. But Jane would have died anyway, from a self-inflicted wound, pints of her blood were spilled out on the floor when she was already weak. Yet Claudia knows her career is over – once was bad enough, but twice she has failed to be vigilant. She hates Alicia with a deadly hatred. Even more, she hates Jane, who has cost her her job.

Ninety-Seven

Ken phones Bruce the next morning.

'Doctor, I'm afraid I have some bad news for you. It's Jane. I'm afraid she died last night; she took her own life, as you said she would.'

' Oh dear.' Silence while it sinks in. 'I knew she planned to . . . How did it happen?'

'We're not sure whether she would have died from her self-inflicted injury – she slashed a vein in her arm again – but there was also a fire in the room. She was in the quiet room, which is where she liked to go to get away from things. We suspect Alicia had a hand in it. I'm sorry, Doctor; it's come as a shock to us all.'

'Yes, I understand. You searched her room after I spoke to you all?'

'Yes – a full search – but nothing was found. It's not always possible to find every tiny item. We think she may have used a pin, or an industrial staple or something. Maybe she hid it in the room until she needed it.'

'I'm very sorry that it should have ended this way, Ken, though I have to say maybe it's a blessing too. I think she thought of little else but dying.'

'Yes, well, it can't be helped. She was always a risk. It doesn't look good for the reputation of the ward, but I don't think we've even had time to get to grips with that one yet.'

'I'd appreciate it if you could let me know about the funeral arrangements, when you know yourselves. I imagine there'll be a post mortem?'

'Almost certainly. We don't know whether any charges will be brought or anything – we're still cleaning up the mess, and to be honest we haven't had time to think about it.'

'I imagine it was a shock for Elsie?'

'Yes. She's taken it hard, she was at home when it happened. But like us, she's not too surprised either. Life goes on.'

'Thanks for letting me know. I'll pop up later and see if there's anything I can do to help – maybe just speak to Elsie or something . . . '

'Fine. Whenever you want. We'll see you later.'

Bruce is sad, but also elated to hear the news. It's what she always wanted, he tells himself. And what choices did she have about her life? None. Yet she exercised the choice to leave it. And he would have taken that option away from her if he'd been able. Something in him senses a triumph here – her secret other life has finally claimed her.

Although this is not how he felt when his mother died, he still feels culpable, still senses the wave of disapproval and anger that is waiting to break over his head, as blame is apportioned and questions asked. He decides to go up to the ward and pre-empt it by offering support.

He knows he will have to provide a report for the coroner and he needs all the support he can get; anger will only get in the way of that, but he feels some anger none the less. How did they let this happen? Why did they not listen more closely to his warning? He feels tugged by many different emotions and decides to find Joe later to talk to about it.

One blessing is that he has no angry relatives to deal with, doesn't have to cover his back in that regard, having warned the staff about Jane's state of mind. But they can't be asked to be with Jane twenty-four hours a day. Still, he knows someone will have to take the blame for it – whoever is most junior, probably, though Bruce knows he will have to tell Dr Khan, and he's not looking forward to that at all.

Ninety-Eight

Bruce, meeting Elsie on the corridor, simply says "I'm sorry" and touches her on the arm. For once, Elsie is pleased to see Bruce. The two of them are the only people who really knew Jane well, the only ones who now share this feeling of personal loss after what has happened.

They stay together while the rest of the staff continue to prepare for the return of the other patients to their own quarters, sorting out their belongings, cleaning up, calming everyone down.

Bruce takes in the news more fully when he passes Jane's room. The door is open and no one has attempted to sort out her things.

An idea comes to Bruce. 'Do you know if Jane left any papers behind? Drawings, writing, anything like that?'

'There are some drawings. She used to do a lot of writing too. I looked at it once but I couldn't make head nor tail of it. I think it was written in some sort of code. I think they'll all be passed to her nearest relative, whoever that is, but I could get them copied and sent to you, if you like.'

'Would it be inappropriate to have a look now? Just to see what's there?'

'I don't suppose anyone will mind. Everyone's pretty busy doing other things.' They go into Jane's room. 'I'll leave you to it.'

'Thanks, Elsie.'

Ninety-Nine

There are three books on the narrow shelf: *Rhyme and Reason*, a poetry anthology for schools, but now out of date, *The Campfire Songbook*, and *Black Beauty*. Bruce glances through them. Would it have helped him to read these books, to understand her better? He doesn't know.

Next to them are seven thick drawing books, standing neatly in line. Bruce opens the first one, cautiously. A skull-like face looks out at him, ringed and criss-crossed in black ink many times. Its hollow eyes and cheeks remind him of Munch's painting of *The Scream*, and they are a poignant reminder of Jane's presence. He is surprised how strong and determined the drawing is. He turns the pages slowly, one by one. There are many faces in the book; some stare accusingly, and some appear both dead and alive, have downcast eyes and hold crucifixes. Symbols of death abound on every page – crosses, hooded figures, gravestones, skulls, all drawn with the same intensity of line and feeling. Primitive, haunting, yet assured in their simple expression, the drawings convey to Bruce a despairing message from a secret world.

Why hadn't he known about these earlier? He knows the answer; he didn't try to find out. He remembers with shame that it was Elsie who'd wanted him to read Jane's file, and that he had only reluctantly agreed. Humbled, he continues to look through the books, noting pages of hieroglyphics – clearly some secret journal that was her only privacy in a world where every move was watched and every mood noted. She had allowed him into that world a little way, to accomplish what she had to do. He decides to make a request to keep the journals and the drawings for further study.

One Hundred

There are inquests – both the coroner's inquest and an internal one. Neither gets to the heart of the matter. Issues to do with staffing levels and fire regulations are brought up.

Claudia does not return to the ward, but nurses her sore lungs and sore temper at home.

The temporary residents leave the next day, and Alicia is kept in solitary confinement. She's too dangerous, though the staff say that if Maureen had been there it would never have happened. Maureen wants to be indispensable but knows she's not. And she didn't know about the lighter, did she? Poor Maureen. She does her best to entertain Alicia, who is singing to herself in her room.

'Jane, Jane go away, come again another day.'

Alicia seems happy.

The staff defend themselves stoutly against the implied criticism that comes their way. Ken should not have allowed Jane to go the quiet room when only he and Claudia were available to invigilate. The camera should have been switched on so that Howard could observe as well as Claudia. Claudia should not have been working so many hours; she was so tired that when she rested for a moment she fell asleep. Alicia should not have been able to get into the room. With Maureen away, Ken should have confined Alicia to her room instead of allowing her to mix with other residents in the TV lounge, with John in charge.

The blame goes round and round until Howard calls the staff together and tells them that there are lessons to be learned, but that everyone did what they could to prevent what happened, and that the time for blame and punishment is at an end. They need to pull together now as a team.

The other residents have gone back to their own hospital, and life will continue as normal. This is stated firmly and clearly, and Bruce hears the message with some relief.

One hundred and one

Elsie is one of the few mourners at the funeral. The staff collected for a wreath, and Elsie asked to go. They were happy to let her represent them.

An elderly aunt is there, but Michelle's children have kept away. Father Dominic, the priest who knew her from her schooldays, has offered to take the service. There is no one else to mourn her.

A tall figure with bloodshot eyes, wearing a dark suit, slips into the crematorium at the last minute. Dr Townsend has come to pay his last respects.

It is a pathetically short and meagre service, but touching in its own way. Bruce finds himself genuinely moved to tears by the simple words of the ceremony. He wishes, as he had with his mother, that there could have been more time. But now there never will be. He sends flowers, knowing somehow that Jane will like them. Alongside the flowers he places a small doll, the one Jane had taken into her sessions with him. It looked pitiful next to the big wreath from the staff, but it is something special, a message about childhood and loss. He leaves it there.

As the mourners exit the chapel, Elsie and Bruce walk side by side, not speaking. Elsie looks pale and it has clearly been difficult for her. Bruce takes her arm.

His mother would have been about her age, he reckons, if she had lived. Elsie glances up at his weary face and pats his hand, comfortingly. They stop to talk to the priest, who is also comforting in his understanding of Jane's troubled life.

'And did the doll mean something to the deceased at all?' he asks in his soft Irish voice.

'It was something she used to represent herself in our sessions together. Herself and other babies she lost.' Bruce feels inadequate in attempting to describe what he'd tried to do.

'Ah, you would be her doctor?' Bruce nods. 'I didn't realise that. I thought you were from the hospital, but I didn't realise you were involved in trying to help her. Of course I know Elsie, we've met before, when Jane was first brought here. Isn't that right?' Elsie nods. 'So what will you be doing with yourself now, Elsie?'

Elsie tells him about her plans for retirement, and her hope that she and Rascal will perhaps do some charity work to help troubled children.

The priest turns to Bruce. 'And yourself? Who will you work with now? Was Jane your only patient on the ward?'

'Yes, she was, as the first part of a pilot study. I think it'll be scrapped now.'

'And why is that?'

'Because I made things worse for her, not better. She killed herself, you know, whatever it says on the death certificate. But maybe you are aware of that.'

'I am, and it's a matter of great sadness to me. But I have to say, it brings me relief as well. The poor woman wanted nothing but an ending to it all, and that's been the way of it for as long as I've known her. All we can do is try. Don't be too hard on yourself.'

He takes their arms and leads them to the old aunt who is waiting by the car.

'I have to drive this lady home, but I'll keep in touch. So long now.'

Elsie and Bruce watch the car drive away and feel suddenly empty and tired. Bruce is thoughtful. 'Maybe we should celebrate somehow, as well as attending her funeral.'

'I can't think how. But she never had fun, you know. I don't think I ever saw her laugh. She was always sad or mad or both.'

'Let's give her a send off all the same. Sometimes death can be something to celebrate. God knows she wanted it enough. Come on, I'll walk you to the pub.'

As he speaks, a flock of nearby wood pigeons clatter up into the sky and make them jump. There is something about the plump, peaceful birds as they circle and come down to land again that is joyful and uplifting.

Together, they stroll towards the bright lights of the Fox and Grapes.

Losing It

About the author

I'm a writer and poet who gained a late MA in Creative Writing at Edge Hill. Trained in psychotherapy, I've worked in Mental Health and allied fields most of my life, having failed to keep order as a teacher and bored to tears by banking, my first two career choices. When not at my computer or kitchen sink, I can be found on my allotment or in the local flea market. I live with my first husband and fourth son in an untidy cottage full of paintings, with a well under the floor and a garden that keeps trying to get into the house.

Other Publications:

A Painting For a Blind Man
A Far Cry.
Mantle Lane Press

The Marsh People.
Victorina Press

Make Up or Break Up,
Overcoming Impotence.
Sheldon

Child With No Name,
What Happened to Selina Smith.
Kindle ebook

The Poison Garden of Dorelia Jones
Immanion Books

A Pint in the Weird-Shit Pub and other tales from the North
Pegasus